SLIM
TARGET

Printed in the U.S.A.

This publication may not be copied in whole or in part, stored or transmitted in any form, electronic or recorded, without permission. Inquiries concerning rights or permissions should be addressed to:

See More Publishing
P.O. Box 6494
Lawrenceville, New Jersey 08648

First Edition Published 2012

Cover Design by Lebbad Design
Text set in 11-point Times New Roman

ISBN-13: 978-0-9883752-0-8
ISBN-10: 0988375206

Dedicated
with
Love and Affection
to
Amy Elizabeth
and
Emily Miriam

SLIM TARGET

S. J. SEYMOUR

Chapter 1

A TELEVISION REPORTER prepared to interview a British bank director on a crisp September morning in the financial district of New York City. She awaited direction from her producer and crew while skimming through multiple sheets of carefully typewritten notes. She intended to ask challenging questions and draw suitable connections between topics.

The eminent bank director stood beside her dressed immaculately in a distinguished pinstripe. He had already firmly shaken the blond reporter's hand with his bony fingers and focused sharply on her bright hazel eyes as they awaited the countdown.

"Biz is an unusual name to have. Not one I often hear," he observed.

"My father liked Biz as a nickname for Elizabeth," she said. "It's short and to the point. And since I cover business news, it's a nice fit for television."

"You've been covering news awhile?" he

asked.

He leaned his tall frame forward as if to get a better view of her.

"Almost a decade," she replied. She retreated somewhat from his steady gaze, and eyed him warily.

Ready, set…for a few final seconds they stood and waited, perfectly in position. Then, with intense focus, Biz's producer turned in her direction.

"Your turn. Take it from here. Five-four-three-two-one."

Biz concentrated her thoughts, raised her chin, faced the camera, and began to introduce her guest live in front of millions of viewers.

"Here on Wall Street with Lord Malcolm Dawson, Director of the London investment bank Hanley's. He helped uncover recent illegal transactions and swiftly brought the perpetrators to justice."

Turning to him, she continued, "Can you tell us if anymore information has emerged on these shocking arrests this morning?"

"I will relay only what I can say with absolute certainty. Police officials delivered summonses to three traders at their business offices at nine in the morning and processed them in district court."

"Can you tell us anything more about the suspects?"

"We can tell you they were trusted employees of Weston & Marks."

A building emblazoned with the Weston & Marks company logo appeared on the teleprompter.

"They had been involved in the merger of the two wireless companies," he continued.

She nodded. "Do you have names we can

provide our viewers?"

"We're not ready to reveal that information at the present time."

She did not allow her impatience to become apparent and pressed on with her questions.

"How were they caught?"

"Our British office in London first noticed significant irregularities in certain transactions at Weston & Marks, along with unusually significant deposits into Swiss bank accounts, and began to investigate three months ago. It took a great deal of time and effort for the discrepancies to be discovered, questioned, and in some cases justified before we could be completely sure of knowing the truth."

"Sir, why, if you were you notified of these ambiguities a matter of months ago, did you not act on the issue until now?"

"We've had our suspicions for some time," he said. "But we could not take strong action until we had evidence. And when we had enough to hold up in court, we moved swiftly."

Lord Dawson continued to gaze directly at her as the heavy camera profiled his beaked nose. Landon, her cameraman, took pictures and videos of them from different angles. In the background, the immense marble Ionic pillars of the New York Stock Exchange loomed symbolically close.

"Do you have anything more to tell us?"

Biz hoped to draw him out and cover as much ground as possible during this fast-paced interview.

"Most of the details are strictly confidential, of course, so can't comment. I can, however, tell you the lead trader, a forty-year-old male, had a career's worth of experience on Wall Street and had signed strict waivers of confidentiality. The other two—his experienced well-paid assistants—had recently spent years in London. I met them. They worked for our company. They were discovered to have broken insider trading rules when they sent disguised information through various electronic channels. Some were even coded within video games." His voice suddenly became weary. "Sadly their plans proved unsuccessful and they were caught."

Biz raised her eyebrow at his use of the word "sadly" but let it go. She could not identify why, but he seemed odd and bothered her. Not that it mattered; it was simply a short interview, but he made her feel uneasy. She sometimes read too much into facial expressions and tried very consciously to not be one of those reporters who overstretch points in their interviews.

"Yes, indeed, what a sad outcome for them and their families," she said. "Thank you very much, Lord Dawson, for answering our questions and for your time."

She smiled at him and they shook hands briefly. They turned around again together to face the camera. She watched Landon focus his lens on her close-up image.

Accuracy in the news business required sharp focus on the facts of the moment without distraction. Her audience expected enlightenment and reactions when they heard news. Viewers needed facts even as they preferred to hope for the best in human nature. But she knew they were all more alike than they were different, and they liked happy endings.

"There you have the latest word from Lord Malcolm Dawson, director at Hanley's, one of

England's largest banks. That's all for now. We hope you can tune in again later for more breaking news of the huge story of the day. Sending it back, live from Wall Street, this is Biz Andrews for WYN-TV, the greatest financial news channel in the business."

The camera panned to a wider view. Fans unable to hear the television interview waved with wild enthusiasm in the background. Cars screeched impatiently as onlookers waved at the cameras. And then the station broke to commercial.

Lord Dawson nodded to his driver. Together they swiftly headed to the impressive black limousine waiting at the curb. Stewart, the driver, opened the door of the passenger seat and Lord Dawson stepped in. The vehicle departed within seconds.

Back on the scene, Biz turned to her friendly coworker who was already rearranging his equipment and packing everything into the van.

"How did it go?"

"Fine," Landon smiled. "Now let's find that new restaurant Jessie recommended."

"Sorry," Biz said. "I still have another report to finish today, and then I'm cutting out early to prepare for my party tomorrow. You'll bring Coretta and the kids, I hope."

"We'll be there."

Landon waved goodbye. Minutes later the entire video shoot had been packed into vans and driven away.

Chapter 2

STEWART GAZED intently ahead along the curving highway. Periodic bursts of pleasure invaded his consciousness as he gulped another pill.

Once he had lived here in New Jersey. Now he only visited America for temporary working visits and entered the country with a forged passport. He worked hard to make his accent sound British but lately he found himself automatically reverting to more natural American inflections. He would have to be careful about that.

Having passed the tunnel under the Hudson River, Stewart listened to the tires of the limousine whistle along the New Jersey freeway. Cars shot past them from behind like bats out of hell speeding who knew where. He had driven this route countless times in the past and kept to a high speed. His job now was to be an excellent limousine driver. He had learned to speed smoothly, take turns slowly, and brake gently.

Dual wipers deftly cleared light drizzle as a brief shower splattered rain the width of the windshield. His lordship had fallen asleep in the rear seat of the limousine, nodding unconsciously in a somnolent trance, his long thin arms relaxed.

"Do it if you want to," Lord Dawson suddenly said from the back seat. Then he fell asleep again.

A British lord by inheritance, Dawson sat on the British Defense Committee in England and had joined a committee having to do with international security although he did not attend the House of Lords more than strictly necessary. He voted in elections and appeared an upright law-abiding member of the House of Lords.

He sometimes told Stewart about himself during their long drives. As a young boy, he had attended an elite well-known boarding school in Somerset. His mother and father had spent years buying land in Asia and were so preoccupied with their own travels abroad that they left him to pursue his own interests with immense freedom. He read classics in foreign languages and knew French, Italian, Spanish, Greek, and some Russian. He had also learned Icelandic, a language unlike any other, during a year in Reykjavik as a teenager. After he took First Class Honors in Classics from the University of London, he trained in a bank.

He expected to meet his second wife in the "City by the Bay." Clare had already arrived from England to visit her son Christopher and maintain and improve her professional connections with the California art world. She owned the Newland Gallery in London named in memory of her late husband.

Lord Dawson, in turn, had inherited a tall stately edifice in Mayfair, a fancy area of London near Grosvenor Square, and made it their primary residence. They spent some weekends at his country house near Blenheim Palace, constructed four hundred years earlier with many buildings of golden Cotswold stone. But Clare rarely visited their other country property in Oxfordshire and left the maintenance to him and his staff, and Lord Dawson did not encourage her interest.

Stewart turned his head to ponder a panoramic view of the city through his side window. He sighed. He had been given official approval.

After thirty minutes, the limousine reached Newark International Airport in Newark, New Jersey. Stewart parked the long vehicle prominently in the arrival concourse at one of the terminals to better display Lord Dawson as he alighted in grand style. Stewart lifted the older man's familiar brown leather suitcase and motioned aside skycaps hoping to make tips. This was a courtesy that Lord Dawson expected. He rolled the large Italian leather case indoors to the airline counter.

Stewart planned to stay behind to take a closer look at Biz and fine-tune his course of action. The two men would meet again in England two weeks later. He would have plenty of time to figure out how to achieve his goals before then.

Chapter 3

AUTUMN LEAVES at their height of color were just beginning to fall in New Jersey. Biz caught herself in a large etched mirror reflected in the late-afternoon sun. She had worn a sleek crimson sheath dress and jacket with matching high heels, certain to attract the eyes of her guests. She had been examining a bouquet of exuberant flowers overflowing a sage green vase set at the center of a large round table in middle of an enormous room.

She had decided to hold this party in an effort to soften her image at the office. And she had made a conscious effort to include a lot of people to ward off any rumors that she might play favorites. A pianist would play classical selections and jazz to lend sophistication to the gathering. An afternoon and evening party with drinks and food on the terrace would please all her guests, she hoped. Maybe, with luck, the wasps would keep their distance from the buffet.

Flipping an errant strand of blond hair across her smooth forehead, she rearranged a variety of orchids thoughtfully placed on other long rectangular tables and sideboards decorated with giant urns. Carefully she surveyed each petal for freshness.

Her first guest arrived. It was Dean, her boyfriend, although lately their relationship had been rocky.

"Thank you for coming," she said. Holding his hand firmly, she gave him a quick peck on the cheek and smiled.

"I'm sorry I couldn't come earlier. I've been at the office. The office manager organized a special celebratory lunch for our clients today."

"That's okay," Biz said. "But it's odd you didn't mention the meeting on the phone yesterday." Nor had he called her all day.

"The business just came up. Associates flew in from out of town. We hadn't been warned."

"Not to worry, I've been super busy," she said and tried to sound soothing and forgiving. "You look great."

Dean had dressed appropriately, in a brown jacket with beige khakis and a green polo shirt, and had obviously polished his shoes until they shone. He didn't return the compliment. Instead he fidgeted nervously then wandered energetically around the enormous ballroom.

More guests began to arrive and she greeted them all with great enthusiasm. Her event would be over in a fleeting few hours, and she had to enjoy the fun now. A few minutes later, Mitch Morris stood smiling at the front door.

Inviting her boss who was head of Morris, Inc. and owner of WYN-TV had been a bold move for her.

"Come in. Have a drink," she said, and gestured around the room. "Do you like the way the club looks since it's been renovated?"

Mitch paused and contemplated the view of the lake and tennis courts. "It's easy on the eyes in here, certainly," he said thoughtfully. "I can't remember how it used to be. I hope the surrounding area is safe enough for you. Are you enjoying yourself?"

"I love Mountain Lakes. It's perfect for me."

"I worry about you living alone."

Her face flushed. She wasn't sure if it was anger or embarrassment. She wanted to say, "Whose fault is it that I'm living alone?" Instead she smiled. "Don't worry, I have a security system on all my doors and at every window. It's as safe as a bank vault. It's absolutely quiet outside, too, except for nature, and that's what I love about it."

"I hope so," he said. "You're one of our most important employees. By the way, excellent work on the insider-trading scandals at Weston & Marks."

He leaned toward her and continued in an intimate tone. "I'm not sure I should be here today."

She nodded but looked away. "Let me introduce you around, although I expect everyone here is already aware of who you are."

"I'm sorry I can't stay long. We'll have dinner soon, you and me. I'll take you on the jet."

She gulped. This was what he always did to rope her back in. She had to stay strong.

"I'd like to introduce you to someone. I have a visitor this week, and I want you to meet him," he said.

Her eyebrows knit briefly in puzzlement.

Exactly at that moment Biz watched a man walk in their direction. He had very straight posture and his smile was wonderfully wicked. She felt a spark of excitement.

Mitch lifted his arm to signal acknowledgement as the new guest joined them. "I take full responsibility for asking him to your party," said Mitch, smiling at their new guest. "Let me introduce Arthur Deephart."

Biz turned to Arthur and smiled invitingly into his eyes.

"Arthur is an artist from whom I've acquired several paintings. We met in England at one of his shows."

"How wonderful," she said. "What brings you to America?"

"I'm here to accept my induction into the American Academy of Arts and Sciences as a Foreign Honorary Member. I have to admit I rarely show my work in the United States. I normally live in London."

Mitch turned to her and said thoughtfully to Biz, "Perhaps you might want to visit his painting exhibit when you're in England. He's also an art theft expert."

"Exactly what I need to learn about." Biz said, and became visibly more alert. "Those recent art heists in Greece and all over Europe have alarmed the art world and I'm interested in learning more about them. My group is about to travel to three European countries."

"Sounds fascinating," said Arthur.

"We plan to interview business officials at a conference in Oxford. In France we'll cover an important meeting of finance ministers near Paris, and in Italy another financial meeting near Rome. We'll also investigate recent art thefts and dig for facts surrounding their disappearances. Maybe we should contact you."

"Please do. And I hope you can stop in at the Newland Gallery while you're in London. I'd be happy to show you some of my paintings."

Biz blushed at the intimate look he gave her, as if he felt entitled to search deeply into her soul.

"We aren't really sure of visiting London, but we may if we have any extra time," she said.

Mitch picked up on the idea without hesitation. "You should meet with Arthur in London. Since he happens to be an international expert, he might be able to advise us on art security issues."

"Okay, I'll email you all about our trip." Then she audibly gasped as he almost kissed her. He warmly shook her hand and held one arm around her shoulder.

As if on cue, Dean walked over to Biz and demonstratively stroked her other arm in an unusual display of affection.

"Would you care to have another glass of sangria?" Dean asked.

"Thanks. I think I'd better not."

She had momentarily forgotten he was there. He had been around Biz since her days at The Belton School. He rivaled Mitch in physical stature and generally left an impression of trustworthy goodness. He was relentlessly polite with her and they had developed a pleasant affable relationship. Although usually preoccupied with his work, he tended to be a safe friend: steady, helpful, and trusted by her parents.

Sometimes, she thought, he had become too

assuming even if she found him reassuring and comforting. While they were by no means securely married, all too often they acted like an older married couple.

Still she dreamed on. She sometimes imagined buying a huge house in Mountain Lakes and having children. At the same time, she knew a woman did not buy a house for herself there, not a never-married thirty-something career woman without children.

She nodded briefly to them and walked in the direction of the buffet feeling a buzz of excitement from the growing crowd. Landon Templeton, her cameraman, brought his wife Coretta, and they joined a conversation with Jessie Forbes, her producer, and Gina Lipper, their young production assistant. One of her favorite cameramen, Luther, came with his wife Marleen. Friends and employees from the office, current and past, helped themselves to satisfying fare at the colorful tables.

Biz walked past Mitch and Arthur and stopped again just long enough to overhear Arthur say, "I'm looking forward to returning to England. While I like America, it isn't as exciting and cultured as I remembered. I believe civility, like fashion, starts first in Europe and travels to the States."

Annoyed, Biz had to keep herself from marching up to Arthur and objecting. Instead she calmed herself and turned her attention to her friends, family, and colleagues. Many had grown up together in Mountain Lakes and had attended the same private school. One, specifically her friend Julie MacMillan, always made her feel saner. They made plans to get together soon, just the two of them. Then she introduced Julie to Landon and his wife and kids. It always warmed Biz's heart to see Landon's tight-knit family.

Soon the evening ended and everyone gave goodbye hugs on their way out. All the guests had left except for Arthur. He lingered by the doorway, then turned to her slowly and lifted up her hands together. "Thank you very much for the party."

"It took a lot of work so thanks for saying that," she said. She appreciated his attention.

"I have to make a call and my cell battery has run down. May I use your phone please?"

"Certainly, here it is," she replied politely and handed him her cell phone. She suddenly felt vulnerable being alone with him in the vast front hall of the club.

After he made his brief call to confirm his room at the hotel, he handed back the phone.

"Thank you, very kind of you," he said charmingly in his English accent as he stopped and shook her hands briefly.

Then he bent over and, with his fingers placed gently on her cheeks, gave her a tender lingering kiss. He walked to the door, flashed his wicked smile, and strolled into the dark night.

She stood rooted in the doorway for a few minutes and gazed after him spellbound. Some part of her remembered he had said unfriendly words about America. She was a journalist and news reporter and had to keep an objective view toward just about everything. But this was her home country and she didn't like hearing it disparaged. If she met him again, she would simply have to make him change his mind.

Chapter 4

A FEW DAYS later, Dean stopped by as he often did after work. He seated himself comfortably on a down sofa next to her fireplace with its elaborate marble mantle and brass andirons. Basking in comfort, he rested his feet on her walnut coffee table heavily laden with travel photography books and magazines.

Meanwhile, Biz was nervously rushing around her kitchen fixing the dinner, almost burning the veal medallions. She had plenty of work from the office she hoped to finish that evening. To be a good financial reporter, she needed precious time to constantly watch and learn more about the financial markets. If she could get Dean to help with the after-dinner cleanup, she could finish her report on a hot new coffee stock. But she wasn't betting on it.

Adding to her pressure, Dean walked into the kitchen and poured wine into her delicate etched wineglasses and gave her a glass. He turned to her, leaned closer, and smiled as he gently lifted and twisted a lock of her hair with his fingers.

Sometimes he signaled to her in this way when he wanted to take a little detour with her in the bedroom before dinner.

She purposely looked busy pouring sauce on the plates because she was. After arranging fennel leaves decoratively, she layered veal with carrot slices on top until he backed off.

They drank wine together as they supped at her dining room table and chatted quietly about the world of business. As usual, Dean discussed practical topics with her, mostly about her accounts, and advised her where he thought she should invest. She always made a concentrated effort to learn more about the stock market and global finances from him. But trying to relax, she was exhausted almost to tears and had to struggle to stay awake.

"Would you like to watch a movie?" Dean asked, sensing her fatigue.

Biz smiled gratefully. "Thanks for asking but I'm just too tired. And I have a report to finish. You could go alone. Honestly, I wouldn't mind."

He left soon after that, annoyed perhaps, and did not help clean up the kitchen.

It was getting more and more like this: working all the time and then finding her down time with Dean disappointing. She had some money but she still needed a great deal more if she wanted complete financial independence. She had heard some people late in life say they wished they had not worked so hard. Though she enjoyed her job, it required a ton of energy and was highly stressful. And she wondered: Is this all there is in life?

Chapter 5

BIZ RETURNED home from work the next day and realized she was missing her cell phone. A great deal of her professional life was invested in her tiny mobile device and she desperately needed to find it. Deciding to drive herself back to the office rather than waiting for her favorite driver, she headed to her car and placed her designer bag on the front seat.

She would simply review her day to remember when her phone had disappeared. As she drove the short distance back to her office, she thought it odd she hadn't noticed her cell phone missing earlier. Usually, it hardly left her side.

As the shadows grew longer that September afternoon, her thoughts grew steadily more apprehensive. She nervously chewed her sugarless gum. Her cell phone held a lot of personal data, her life, as she reminded everyone. With all the excitement about her trip to Europe, her cell phone must have slipped her mind. Yes, she considered, she was just preoccupied. Her cell phone had to be at the office.

As she approached the large building where she had an office at WYN-TV, her thoughts drifted to Dean. They had always been physically attracted to each other. Her parents liked him. She could tell they wanted her to be happy and perhaps get married. But she and Dean had taken to passing each other almost like ships in a harbor on the subject of marriage.

She mused about her parents, especially her mother whose life she admired. They had remained loving partners: open-minded, well-traveled, confident, and secure. They were cautious and more predictable than Biz. And they had a dynamic relationship with plenty of open and honest communication. They had each other's unconditional love. There was much about their lifestyle Biz respected as she gazed with uncertainty into her own future.

She was so lost in thought she did not notice the car behind her. Every time she took a turn, she was being followed.

Chapter 6

STEWART'S SUBCOMPACT blended in with the others in the parking lot. The out-of-state license plate and decals on the windows signaled its origins and current use as a rental vehicle but it did not appear unusual in its current location or attract any attention from security in the publicly accessible lot.

He adjusted his thick glasses and pulled his blue cap over his ears. He planned to have laser surgery to correct his vision during this trip. Just one more step in the long process of altering his appearance.

First, he had a job to finish, and he had brought along his blue baseball hat for good luck. He would wait here for his chance all night if he had to.

He had often thought each time would be his last working for the Diamondbacks. But before long, he was once again donning face masks, attacking security systems, and stealing jewelry and paintings. This time would be different. He was at work on his own project.

Chapter 7

BIZ PAUSED to catch her breath as she passed through a company security check. In the front lobby, Mitch headed in her direction. She stopped to speak to him.

"I went by your office just now and asked after you," Mitch said as he gave Biz an appreciative look.

She knew by now that she was not the first female anchor to catch his roving eye and she felt immensely shamed for having fallen for his flattery.

"I've misplaced my cell phone. Have you seen it, by any chance?"

"I meant to warn you," Mitch said casually. "The battery on my own cell phone ran down and when I saw yours on your desk, I borrowed it. Had to make some calls right away and forgot to return it when I went for lunch. It's back on your desk."

"You took my phone? I just came all the way back to the office for it." She paused in a bid to control her rising anger. "Thanks for letting me know where it is," she rushed off with a wave of her arm.

"Sorry, we'll talk soon. Promise." Mitch said longingly as he gazed after her.

As Biz walked toward her office, Gina looked up from her computer and nodded. Gina helped her organize research for her news reports and helped Jessie, her producer, with details they needed to produce the show. The producer researched companies as needed and coordinated various moving parts.

They would soon accompany her to Europe. Gina was excited about it, and constantly reminded her of the trip. There were details to work out, commitments, research, and travel to keep her busy.

Taking the stairs as usual, Biz rushed around the office while attempting to remain cool and confident at the same time. She kept thinking of Mitch. She had so much confidential data on her cell phone and always needed it with her. Certainly, in rare instances, Gina had picked up her phone to synchronize calls with her. But never before had anyone borrowed it without her permission. How could he have done it? Then again, when she thought about it, he had a history of taking what he wanted regardless of the consequences.

She reached her office and gazed around her familiar bookshelves and desk with its collection of interesting photos and unique tiny boxes. She found her cell phone at the corner of her desk, turned it on, and checked her call log. Only three recent calls had been logged. She slipped her phone and a few books and folders into her bag, and left the office for the second time that day.

Chapter 8

BIZ TURNED her car onto a state route still busy with rush-hour traffic. After passing neighboring villages, she made a turn onto the Boulevard in the Borough of Mountain Lakes. A short commute away from a major international metropolitan center, the town attracted wealthy exurbanites with the promise of a healthy lifestyle in an uncrowded setting. It consistently provided various safety and educational benefits that its fortunate residents valued.

New Jersey had a well-known image problem as the most maligned in America. Of course, to Biz that did not matter. She loved her home state. She raised her head to the cloudless sky and smiled in delight when she saw two hot air balloons in the sky. She had once rewarded herself with a trip in one with Dean and had the photos to prove it.

An hour later, she had dinner with Dean as usual. Tonight he seemed in a good mood and was trying to be helpful. Afterwards, he leaned over to give her a kiss, then climbed a ladder to re-hang one of her favorite landscape paintings. He stopped briefly to scrutinize markings on its back.

He said, "This picture is marked with a logo inside checkerboard squares. Do you have any idea why?"

"No, I don't, and not a single person at the auction house could explain the sign to me either," she said.

"Where did you buy it?"

"In the city. In my early days as a reporter I covered a gallery opening," she said standing behind him, "Since art prices soared for European paintings, I was preparing a report about the art world. That piece didn't have the highest price of all the paintings at the show but I liked it and it's grown on me even more since I bought it. I love the clean classic lines. And it's very old, I think. The frame appears much newer. Maybe it used to be larger. The sides were folded into the frame. It strikes me as odd, and always has."

"It's a very fine painting," Dean agreed. He turned to give her another kiss.

"It reminds me of a genuine Old Master painting. Everyone who has seen this piece has assumed it cost me an outrageous amount. But most of the others at the show were more expensive."

As Dean straightened the freshly re-hung painting, the security alarm sounded.

Chapter 9

STEWART SAT and waited in the white car, and kept an eye on her townhouse. In the twilight he made notes, drew diagrams of her home by hand, and took multiple photographs. He would have to wait until after dark to leave the subcompact unless he stretched out and slept there. Alone with his thoughts, he began to seethe.

Finally, the darkness closed in, enough to provide him with cover. Hidden by trees, he crept stealthily through bushes and peered furtively through her living room window.

Stewart watched the couple kiss each other under the chandelier. The man, apparently Biz's boyfriend, climbed a ladder to re-hang a vast oil painting. Stewart recognized the masterpiece he had once stolen and shook his head at the irony.

Stewart took one step back when the burglar alarm sounded. Then he fled and crouched in some nearby boxwoods and yew bushes. He sprinted further through prickly bushes into the woods.

Biz flipped on her outside light, and called

Dean to investigate. They went outside to look around but by that time, Stewart was nowhere to be found. After a short time, they returned indoors.

That must be her boyfriend's name, he thought. He was angry with himself and his muscles ached from crouching. He slithered into his hidden car and lay under a blanket in the back seat and waited.

Tonight would not be the night. No, not until she was alone. The police finally drove past and didn't take notice of his car if they saw it. He counted this bit of luck as a good sign. He would certainly need a lot more of it.

Chapter 10

THE NEXT WEEKEND, Biz and Dean carved a few hours from their busy schedules to take a long-awaited hiking trip in northwest Jersey. There were many well-tended state parks to visit in the Garden State. Biz especially wanted to show Dean a surprise at the top of one of the higher mountains.

They drove north for an hour Saturday morning until they reached the state park. He parked his Porsche in the graveled lot. They donned heavy jackets, tied on their hiking boots, and applied sunscreen directly on each other's noses.

After they left the car, they worried whether they had bothered to lock it. Neither could remember but they both assumed they had. With no one else around, they trusted it would be safe to leave it.

A notice board mapped the trails currently open in the park indicating where exactly they would be free to navigate that day. A route they chose marked in green had a well-trodden granite trail. They hiked along wide gravel footpaths and marveled at the gorgeous scenery. Golden leaves swished past them and crackled at their feet. Flocks of migrating birds twittered, and from high in the sky, sharp sunlight filtered in rays of dusty particles through the heavily wooded terrain. Formed from glaciers, impressive boulders bordered their trailer-width lane on both sides. Occasionally, stair steps built into the hills made of chiseled granite gradually rose and lifted them higher.

The long climb made them both feel energized. Biz could sense herself feeling more oxygenated with every step. Finally, after an hour of climbing with the aid of painted wooden markers, a signpost announced they had almost reached the summit.

"This is excellent exercise," Dean said.

"I couldn't agree more," said Biz.

Dean wasn't the most stimulating conversationalist but he had given his time and effort to her, and for that she felt grateful.

After a few minutes' rest, he said thoughtfully and somewhat formally, "I wanted to tell you, I thought your party went very well."

She paused to lace her shoes. "Thanks. That means a lot. I just hope everyone had a good time."

They walked around a giant granite boulder and commented on the charcoal and ashes remaining from little fires hikers had recently built.

"Other hikers have evidently been here, and not very long ago," he remarked as he walked uphill behind her.

"I used to come here with my hiking club when I was in college."

The path rounded another corner and passed a few boulders. They paused at a sign marker.

"Not bad. We've climbed nearly two thousand

feet," Dean read proudly.

Biz turned and looked searchingly at Dean and all around, sharing a smile of achievement. Behind him, a sight she had been waiting to see positively enthralled her.

"Look," Biz said. "It's a mirror image today."

A small quiet lake situated at a relatively high elevation for New Jersey provided a welcome destination. The trees were reflected, in the perfect stillness of the water beneath, in symmetry.

They walked around the lake silently. Passing massive stony chunks of granite, they gazed at awesome views, highly defined in bright sharp sunlight. At the end of the path, they stopped at a clearing encircled with a low fence and Dean read his map.

He smiled at her. "It's called Surprise Lake."

"Surprise? I always wondered what it was called." She smiled. "I love it. This has to be one of my favorite places in all of the East Coast. And unfortunately, I don't get here often enough. Not many park visitors can say they've hiked this high to see the view. It extends for miles, doesn't it? That's the New York skyline in the distance. Once upon a time we could have seen the Twin Towers from here."

As she gazed at the view, she made a positive effort not to feel dizzy. She motioned to an area behind her where she wanted to sit: a place between boulders that might actually be a cozy warm place out of the wind to cuddle for awhile. She would not have minded where that might lead.

Dean suddenly turned around. "It's a great view but we should head back."

"What for?"

"I planned to meet someone later today."

"Who do you plan to meet?" she asked sadly as they started hiking back down the steep rocky trail.

Dean seemed unsure of what to say. "I have to head into the office."

"On a Saturday?"

"Janice said there are some papers she needs signed."

Janice, his office manager, almost lived at the office. Biz knew this. She also knew that Dean had been spending more time at the office since Janice and he started working together.

She stretched her neck and turned up her nose into the sunlight. She did not question him further.

Chapter 11

AFTER BIZ and Dean left the parking lot, Stewart decided to grope his way through the car and see what he would find. He had followed the couple all the way to the remote park.

He had taken a couple of days to regroup. The security alarm going off had put the fear of being caught by the police into him. He had cut it too close. Time was running out. He would have to think this through better and be more careful.

The parking lot was completely deserted but still he approached the Porsche cautiously and inspected it like a man fascinated by powerful cars. When he realized no one was around, he took out the long wire that he would use to unlock the doors. He was in luck. On closer inspection, he saw something that made him chuckle…They had forgotten and left the car unlocked.

He put his hand to the door handle. How convenient it was, to not have to wear gloves. When he had started his job with the Diamondbacks he had used them for petty thefts and such, but did not need them anymore: a drug he had taken had smoothed his fingertips. He knew he would not leave any fingerprints.

Stewart could not find anything useful in the car he wanted until he discovered Biz's handbag. In it, her daily planner had details of all her most private information, her phone numbers, and her itinerary—all the private information he needed.

He grabbed the planner immediately when three cars full of preoccupied teenagers arrived in the parking lot. He closed the doors casually and strolled out of sight, his day's work accomplished.

Chapter 12

THEY DROVE along the highway back to her house in Mountain Lakes in uneasy silence, neither one saying a word. Biz was hoping the trip would lend itself to some show of emotion but Dean still said nothing. Thinking about her schedule, Biz checked the inside pockets of her bag and noticed her brush, her wallet, nothing amiss, except...

"Where's my planner?"

"Maybe you left it at home."

"I always carry it with me in case I need to add something. It holds my entire European itinerary, the hotels I'll stay in, flights I'll take, that sort of thing." The information was on her computer, but she also liked to carry one around and write in it. Her private journal was her repository of personal impressions and secret notes. Sometimes, it calmed and comforted her for purely emotional reasons.

"Why would you bring something so important to go hiking?"

She recoiled. He had grown colder, probably knowing he had disappointed her, and he immediately went on the defensive. She could tell he felt preoccupied with work or Janice or perhaps both, and felt nauseated wondering if anything more personal was happening. She had to assume it might be. He made her worry.

She thought with nostalgia of the strawberry festivals in the Pennsylvania countryside she and Dean had visited a few years ago and the annual Shad Festival by the bridge in Lambertville. She had enjoyed the hot air balloon festivals, aerial stunts they had seen at air shows, and horse carriage tournaments they had attended. She could tell they definitely would not visit any teddy bear picnics for kids in the near future. She could not express, even to herself, how sad that conclusion made her feel.

She thought of her college friend Tina, married with a four-year old, successfully continuing her career as a doctor. She also thought about an always kind and light-hearted aunt of hers who had never had children. She wondered who of the two was more satisfied with her life. Either way, thinking of them being happy, whether married or unmarried gave her strength. She needed to take control of her own destiny. It was time.

"Dean, we need to talk."

"Is it something we can discuss later? We're both so tired from hiking," he said speeding up the car.

"I think now is as good a time as any."

"Okay, fine. Janice gave me a few bad stock tips. They tanked and she's leaving the firm."

"What?" Biz turned to him in surprise. This was not where she thought the conversation would lead.

"Some of my clients have taken me to court."

"How could you have made such an error and taken stock tips from Janice? She's an office manager not a broker."

He looked away uncomfortably and she knew what the answer was. It was because he would probably do just about anything Janice asked him to.

"I'm very sorry for the trouble you're in. I had no idea. But we talk every day. I can't believe you didn't tell me."

He continued to say nothing.

She sighed. "Look, for some time I've been thinking we need to take some time apart."

Dean said nothing. In fact, he continued in stony silence until he dropped her off at her townhouse unnecessarily early for a Saturday afternoon. He leaned over and gave her a kiss out of habit.

"I hope you'll reconsider," he said with strange, almost dead calm.

Just like that, it was over. No argument, no tears, no recriminations.

"Goodbye," she said and closed the car door.

She was fully conscious of being at least temporarily relieved of another source of pressure in her life.

Chapter 13

BY SUNDAY afternoon Biz's relief had diminished, replaced by an overwhelming sense of sadness about ending her long-term relationship with Dean. She would spend the afternoon and evening with her parents and her best friend Julie. And that thought sustained her through the weekend.

As she drove to her parent's house, her teenage and college years crept into her conscious thoughts. She contemplated what she would have done differently. It was all part of her past. There was nothing she could do anymore to change it. She mused on a suggestion she had heard: we can only do what we feel is best with the information we have, as incomplete and flawed as it might turn out to be.

Her constituency of television viewers, her fans, expressed appreciation of her work, liked watching her, and wanted her to stay on or so she believed. She enjoyed her success, as ephemeral as it was. Still, being unmarried and living for herself

occasionally caused her anguish. Society liked
certainty and she was not any different. She could
only hope her romantic life would improve.

After the BMW rolled through a couple of
green lights, the road narrowed. A few cars
followed Biz. An ambulance siren passed but not
unusual traffic, she thought. She opened the roof of
her car and the windows to let in fresh breezes after
a recent rain shower. She drove quietly along a few
more leafy country lanes until she reached her
parents' historic estate. Similar properties outside of
towns like Mountain Lakes and the great suburban
sprawl were originally self-sufficient farmsteads.
Although not large anymore in the context of the
American West, farm owners often raised cows,
sheep, and horses, and supplemented their efforts
with profitable professional businesses. With the
countryside gradually developing in chunks, most
of the oldest farms had changed hands and
downsized over time as housing developments
overran neighboring land.

Biz passed Hardscrabble Road, so named for
generations of farmers who had been working the
fertile soil for hundreds of years. A stone barn
converted to a small museum, open to the public
daily, held a baptismal gown her grandmother had
saved for posterity and ultimately donated to the
museum for a pioneer exhibit. The baby gown
strongly reminded her in miniature of the wedding
gown she dreamed of wearing one day. Her mother
had carefully stored a long wedding dress of her
grandmother's made of Belgian lace to hand down
in the family, but it was too large for Biz. As the
sunny golden shadows that late afternoon
lengthened, she approached Nassau Park. An idyllic

green square faced a pond with a bridge a short way from the driveway of the Andrews' family estate.

The familiar dignified green sign engraved in gold letters announced the entrance to Warm Springs Farm outside of Morristown. Two pillars carved with stone pineapples on top symbolized hospitality. Wrought iron railings connected them, artistically twined together with decorative ivy leaves. The splendid paved driveway was lined with London plane trees and mature English boxwoods.

Biz finally pulled her sports car to a gentle pace and closed the windows. She heard the familiar crunch of tires as she parked in the gravel and flagstone parking area next to her father's larger BMW and her mother's Mercedes. The property had always appeared Old World and grandly opulent to Biz. Her own smaller home in Mountain Lakes comforted her, too, and ultimately was far easier to maintain.

Unnoticed by Biz, a white subcompact had followed her all the way there and inconspicuously parked opposite the end of the estate's driveway behind a thick grove of leafy bushes and holly trees.

Biz left her car doors unlocked and reveled in the peacefulness of the countryside as the unexpectedly giant orb of the gold sun began to set through the trees. Walking to the spacious beautiful house her parents had renovated, she exhaled with relief. No matter how elaborate her life outside of work became, every time she visited her parents her spirits lifted.

She ascended the well-trodden stairs constructed of chiseled slabs of stone. She relaxed as she entered the familiar and beloved entry alcove. Only Foxy, their Finnish Spitz, greeted her at the door. This meant her parents were in the indoor pool at the back of the house.

She placed a box of her mother's favorite fancy chocolates on a highly polished table. She adored the way her mother had furnished the house. Antique furniture and colorful carpets decorated interiors spaces with historic paint colors and gleaming hardwood floors. And traditional flowery chintzes finished sofas and windows in a timeless fashion. She walked into the vast updated country kitchen replete with granite countertops. Welcoming aromas emanated from the oven where a sizzling pot roast and delicious baked potatoes steamed.

She would join her parents for dinner later, but first she wanted to work out. She was still pulsing with nervous energy from work. She decided to take an invigorating run through Nassau Park. She would have just enough time to run before the sun set if she hurried. Donning her running gear, she sprinted along the driveway with great speed and grew puzzled. A white car was parked near the entrance in a grove of trees and had a perfect view of her parent's estate. She wondered whether the owner was lost but cautiously declined to ask.

Chapter 14

STEWART REMAINED waiting inside the subcompact, patiently biding his time. He could see her running, and just watched and waited. The entire vista appeared incredibly lovely. He opened his windows and smelled freshly-mown grass and fragrant flowers. The colors reminded him of rose gold jewelry the color of her watch as she ran past. He was exhilarated to be at such close range to his slim target.

He would have done anything to live there now. A part of him ached as he gazed longingly across the stubbly well-kept fields late on that golden fire-hued afternoon. Cottony clouds the colors of rose quartz filled the deepening sky.

He had been raised in a poor section of the inner city of Jersey City. His warm and large family, the Terrinos, had constant worries about money. Back then he had been known to everyone as Vince, or sometimes to his family as Vinnie.

His father, a gruff man, had nudged him to get out of the house and make something of himself and helped him a little to pay for his filming, camera, and sound engineering courses. His parents hoped television would be a lucrative career and he hoped so, too. He fondly remembered the old tools of his television trade: film slates, shoulder-mounted cameras, microphones, and sound amplifiers.

He remembered how he married his lovely high school sweetheart, Darla, and together they had raised three kids. As soon as they entered school, his wife took a job in a ladies dress shop to make more money. When WYN-TV hired him he held high hopes of climbing the corporate ladder. As his kids grew, the family absolutely needed more income. They were falling behind and he could not keep up with his neighbors. His wife understood his drive and supported his job search, agreeing they could use the money. And so he had begun his search for more lucrative employment.

He kept thinking about his kids. Being back in the same state with them was excruciatingly painful. He followed them on the internet but dared not venture any closer. He might not be able to rein in his desire to speak to them and his secret identity would be blown. For the foreseeable future, they had to believe he had drowned in the ocean after being freed.

Mercifully, his time here was limited. Soon he would return to England. Lord Dawson and the Diamondbacks awaited him.

Chapter 15

BIZ TURNED around and checked the lane. When the car did not follow her, she relaxed a little and tried to shrug off her worries. A fast jogger by nature, she kept up a good pace and planned her exact route ahead. Jogging helped her breathe more easily. She had to be fully in control of her breathing and posture for television. Breathing well had always been a useful skill as she braced herself to give a newscast, just as singing had been a good skill to practice years earlier.

As she ran past green fields and pebbly brooks on the familiar well-trodden footpath, she enjoyed breathing in the fresh air. The warm golden sun that late autumn afternoon spread long gentle shadows. In a Washington art gallery, an area artist had written on a painting: God truly smiled on these fields. She had to agree as she gazed fleetingly at a crabapple tree on one side of her. A bird trio of blue jays, cardinals, and goldfinches energetically fluttered their wings.

The white car remained parked for mysterious

reasons when she returned near the entrance to Warm Springs Farm. A man in the front seat scribbled furiously in a notepad and did not seem to notice her.

She was about to approach and ask if he was lost and then thought better of it, avoided him and went around the back of the property. For some reason, she sensed danger.

She consciously increased her running speed and sprinted without stopping, taking the long way back, out of eyesight of the strange man. With one shoelace untied, she raced inside Warm Springs Farm just as the front doorbell rang.

Chapter 16

BIZ BREATHED a long sigh of relief and embraced her friend Julie in a friendly greeting at the door.

"Thanks for inviting me over."

They walked into the warm pool area. Biz's parents had just cleared out and headed upstairs to dress for dinner. In good spirits, the two friends stepped into the hot tub for a dip.

"You seemed a little nervous when you opened the door," said Julie.

"Oh, it's nothing. I just spooked myself about a car at the end of the driveway. Tend to do that a lot lately. Anyway, tell me what you've been up to."

"I'm much more interested in hearing from you about Arthur Deephart. At your party, I saw him staring at you. A lot."

Consciously keeping her tone casual Biz said, "I might visit him in England. Mitch asked me to use him as a consultant on a story. And I might visit the Newland Gallery where he currently has a show."

She hoped Julie would not ask her anything else about Arthur, remembering the aftermath of the party when he had kissed her.

"What an odd coincidence," said Julie.

"What is?"

"The name Newland. Christopher Newland happens to be the name of a computer scientist I'm going to be working with soon in California. He's a good friend. Not that there's likely any connection."

"This hot water feels great, doesn't it? It's refreshing to kick back for a little while," said Biz.

"I think it's healthy to take time to just meditate about life," Julie said.

Biz made a sound of agreement as they relaxed on the tiled steps inside the vigorous tub.

"My work life can be tiring," said Biz. "I have to aim for perfection every time I stand in front of a camera. And it's super stressful to do fast-paced broadcasts in real time. I have to write a good news summary and look perfect when I deliver it. Those insider-trading cases took hours to investigate. I've interviewed heads of all kinds of companies, banks, hedge funds. And I have to keep up with all of them, too."

Jill nodded, and her arms made waves inside the foaming water.

"But one of my major challenges is being one of the most public faces of WYN-TV," said Biz. "It's not like fame runs in my family. This is all new to me. I think it makes me really self-conscious about my life and choices. Like everyone's watching me."

"I've never really thought about it but that makes sense."

Biz sighed. "Do you feel overextended, too?"

Julie nodded. "Absolutely. Thankfully, I don't have any sort of celebrity to maintain, just a huge work overload. My job has definitely changed since I began to work there after I finished my degree, oh, six years ago. There are changes we make almost every day. I've had to be very flexible. Lately since our mapping application company merged, we've created some efficiencies of scale. But we have plans to expand and that creates human issues. I can't solve everyone's problems," she said, "and I need to cultivate patience when others respond more slowly than I'd like. I think I'm good at making people feel safe talking to me about any of their concerns and I think that is very important, that aspect of having free speech in the workplace. It shouldn't just be a dream."

"Do you still enjoy working there?"

"I suppose being employee number three does have its merits," Julie answered with a wry smile. "I took this job originally when the company started. Many of the earlier employees left. I've just stayed along with the founders and taken on more tasks. The show keeps going and they keep paying and promoting me with better titles. The challenge we're constantly facing is innovating new projects to create more jobs and being efficient. I have enough work to keep me busy every weekend. I'm not sure how I'd fit more into my life anyway. I'm not one of these women with everything together."

"What has the company focused on lately?" Biz asked, unable to help going into reporter mode.

"We've started making new mapping applications in development and marketing. The programs start small and if they're good they're bought by larger companies. My job is to explore the wider theoretical concepts behind the programs when I have time."

"It's private. It's hard to find out," said Biz. "Is it making money?"

"Fortunately, the company is extremely profitable. While it has a terrific future, the owners have the most at stake. If it ever goes public I could do all right. I suppose if Columbia or Stanford were to offer me a job, I might consider it. Otherwise I'm not sure I'd change anything in my life. My little townhouse is comfortable and efficient. It's fine. I suppose my love life is the major aspect of my life I'd like to improve."

"How's that?" asked Biz.

"Well, for example, I think Edward and I will attend a late movie tonight, probably with all males in the audience, to see some fantasy-action-thriller. I'll probably sleep through it. Sound exciting?" Julie paused then gazed at Biz.

"Not so much. I know exactly what you mean. You want someone who's better than good enough," Biz said, hoping to mask the sadness in her voice.

"Speaking of which," said Julie, "How's Dean? I was thinking of having him invest some money I just inherited from my grandparents."

"Investments are exactly what he does," said Biz evasively. "He files my taxes."

"But he's more than a tax preparer to you," Julie smiled knowingly.

The smile faded from her face as Biz said, "No, not anymore."

Julie murmured her support with expressions of sympathy. "When did it happen? Why didn't you call and tell me?"

"It just happened yesterday."

"I didn't know, honest. You've been with him so long. We'll see what happens," said Julie thoughtfully as she sipped her drink. "This wine is good. I'd better not drink too much."

Biz sat up, reached over and passed around towels. "I think we've had enough of this bubbly frothiness," she said as she held out her fingers to inspect them. "My skin's dried like a prune."

After the dinner concluded and Julie had left, Biz walked into her father's study and reclined sleepily with her feet elevated in one of his leather chairs. She wanted to stay longer and hide within its roomy depths.

Richard Andrews sat in a chair near her and picked up a book.

"Since you notice details that others miss, I wonder, have you noticed a white car with a driver parked at the end of the driveway?" Biz said.

"I hadn't actually." Richard looked at her with surprise and concern. "Why? Would you like me to call the police?"

"Don't bother. I saw it hours ago and just wondered. Has it been there any other time?"

"Absolutely not. At least not that I've seen. If it's bothering you then we should report it to the police at once."

She inspected her recently manicured nails. "Maybe I'm imagining it but I can't shake the odd feeling I'm being watched and followed."

"Has anything else happened to make you suspicious?"

"It's just, my burglar alarm went off recently for no reason when Dean was with me."

"Does your security system work? Maybe it needs to be inspected."

"I suppose I should call the security company. I haven't had it checked lately. And then yesterday while Dean and I were hiking, we left his car doors unlocked by mistake and I think someone may have stolen my daily planner. I've carefully searched through nearly everything I own. I can't imagine why anyone would want it."

"That's odd," he said.

"I don't think we need to call the police." After a few moments of silence she asked, "But would you mind if I sleep here tonight?"

"Of course not," he said with his usual affection.

"Thanks. With the trip to Europe coming up next week, I feel more stressed than usual. We're going to uncover a bunch of art heists, or at least try to."

"As a matter of fact, I prosecuted a case with a member of a crime syndicate called the Diamondbacks about eight years ago. I've learned a great deal about art heists." He dug around inside his desk and pulled out an old file containing a picture of a husky Italian man with thick glasses.

"I remember him," she said.

"These recent thefts in Europe resemble my case in one important feature. The Diamondbacks usually left their symbol at crime scenes as a sign they were involved."

"What did it look like?" she asked with interest.

"It was a four-sided shape with a black and white checkerboard inside and a gold logo. That insignia in the center was eye-catching. In my case, the guilty party escaped. Just before the sentencing hearing, he was freed by his accomplices, these so-called Diamondbacks, from his jail cell. They broke barriers and helped him escape. In retrospect, he should have been far more heavily guarded and locked up. If my memory serves me correctly, a boat his conspirators were thought to have used after he escaped held signs from the Diamondbacks. That's how we noticed the connection. All the passengers were presumed lost at sea in a storm near Boston and never found."

"That's fascinating. What if that criminal hadn't drowned?" Biz asked.

"It's unthinkable he survived. We think it's impossible," Richard asserted.

"I'll certainly keep it in mind and let you know if I find out anything about the Diamondbacks in Europe."

"We need to know more about them but it sounds like an extremely dangerous mission. You'd better be very careful. I hope and trust the station is watching out for you. Well, I suppose I'll take my book to bed and say goodnight."

"Wait," she sighed. "There's something else I need to tell you."

Her father appeared instantly uncomfortable, perhaps sensing important news to come as he listened attentively.

"It's Dean. He's been a good steady boyfriend and he's probably what you and Mom consider husband material. Trouble is, I've been having my doubts about him for awhile." She tried to sound casual but was unable to carry it off. "In fact, we broke up the other day after we went hiking. He just wasn't making me happy. I need to apologize to you."

Finally, the tears she had been holding inside

could not be put off any longer. She helped herself to a box of tissues.

"Why?" her father asked sympathetically.

"You and Mom have both invested so much time getting to know him. And it scares me to cut my losses and let you know. Dean and I have been together quite a few years but the way he's been acting lately… Please tell Mom for me?"

He came over and hugged her.

"Of course, I will. You don't need to apologize. It's not up to us to tell you who you should be with. Dean's all right but he's not the only person out there. We'll go along with whoever makes you happy."

She felt intensely grateful for his priceless emotional support. She considered it unlikely she could match her parents' long marriage with one of her own in her lifetime but at least she had great parents. As she thought of this, an image of Arthur kissing her at the party rose unbidden to her mind.

Chapter 17

BIZ TELEPHONED the security system company for a service check the next day. In the late afternoon, the technicians inspected it and gave her an update by phone at the office.

"You can be glad we went there today, Ms. Andrews," said the husky-voiced man from the security company. "Your security system didn't work well when we tested it. It had been tampered with but it held up. When intruders want to enter sometimes they can do enough harm to disable it and they do it so they can have inside access; not the kind of access you want. After that, the system had grown weak from soaking rain. It's good you called for service. It's a 'specially strong system but it needed to be fixed."

She shivered and worried someone had been messing around with her system. She felt terribly lonely and frightened. This was one of those times she did not want to be alone. She would have truly appreciated having someone live with her, and decided to call Julie. She knew she would feel better talking about it.

Julie was already in California for her meeting with Christopher Newland.

"How's the weather?" Biz asked when her friend picked up.

"It's always perfect here in Palo Alto," Julie said warmly. "I had a great dinner last night with my associate Chris Newland. I mentioned you'd be visiting the Newland Gallery in London. And he told me it happens to be his mother's, if you can believe that. She opened it after she moved to England permanently and married that English banker you interviewed, Lord Dawson."

"That's a strange coincidence."

"Indeed. He's traveling to Greece in the New Year and he's asked me to go with him."

"Lord Dawson?"

"No, Chris, of course."

"Oh, that's much better." Biz laughed, and so did Julie. She would not tell Julie that Lord Dawson had troubled her.

"Didn't you say you'd be visiting Greece soon?" Julie asked.

"We will indeed," said Biz. "I'll be searching for information about art thefts that have happened recently in Europe. A syndicate of thieves, specifically a network called the Diamondbacks, has taken responsibility for a giant theft in Athens. They stole an entire collection of ancient artifacts."

"Sounds wild. You'd better watch out."

"I know but it can't be helped. Greece is an extremely beautiful country. Why don't you take the trip with Chris and have a vacation. Maybe we could meet then."

"I can't decide, I don't know yet if I'm going.

Do you assume a guy is serious if he invites you to go on vacation with him? He seems like someone I'd like to know better but it wouldn't be what I'd call a practical relationship. He lives in California. And he's agreed to come to my New Year's Eve party since he'll be in the area for a conference the next week."

"Great!" exclaimed Biz. "I'll get to meet him."

"We also talked about Arthur since he attended your party and we'd both met him. I mentioned you said Arthur would be showing his paintings at the Newland Gallery. Chris told me Arthur is from a very aristocratic family. But I assume you were already aware of that morsel of information?"

"No, I most definitely did not know that, although I had my suspicions." Biz would not talk about Arthur. "On an unrelated topic, do you remember that suspicious vehicle I told you about at the end of the driveway at my parent's house?"

"Of course, I remember. Did you call the police?"

"I didn't," said Biz. "I now wonder whether it could have been related to the theft of my daily planner. Maybe I'm being followed. Do you suppose someone could have followed us hiking and wanted something of mine? Or was I just in the wrong place at the wrong time again?"

"Let's not unite the two and imagine some stalker went after you personally and masterminded a theft. I've heard most of them are simple crimes of opportunity. If thieves find something they want, they just take it."

"I hope you're right. Someone recently tampered with my home security system."

"Well, that is something else. Call me if

anything else happens out of the ordinary. If it worries you at all or doesn't feel right I would suggest you immediately call the police. Tell them everything."

Chapter 18

BIZ PACKED for her trip to England, France, and Italy. She tried to banish thoughts of the unpleasant incidents of the past few weeks as she headed off to Newark International by limousine.

She boarded the plane with her coworkers and watched outside as it taxied onto the runway and waited. Their plane waited for a quarter of an hour in a long line of flights. Finally, it reached the end of the longest and busiest runway, revved the engines, accelerated for takeoff, and soared smoothly into the clear pastel blue autumn sky.

She was thrilled to experience the high altitude ride and then land somewhere else completely different. She liked everything about it: the food, the air whistling through vents, bells pinging mysteriously, doors closing loudly. None of it bothered her. She felt optimistic and happy. Whatever alarmed her back home would not likely continue while she was on another continent. Her mindset relaxed as the plane flew over the Atlantic Ocean and on to Heathrow Airport.

Jessie, Landon, and Gina sat near Biz. They read and chatted happily around her. She felt truly grateful for the trip. Normally a restless sleeper, she drifted into light somnolence aided by the steady hum of the powerful jet engines. After a few hours of sleep she enjoyed watching the rising morning sun in a new rosy-golden dawn.

At Heathrow Airport, the bulky airliner taxied in to park on an apron at one of the terminals. Biz silently recited names in her mind of her favorite areas of London: Old Bond Street, New Bond Street, Oxford Street, Mayfair, Piccadilly, and Sloane Square. She hoped to get to a few of them but first the group planned to visit Oxford. She needed to question some economists from the business school at the University of Oxford.

In the terminal, they waited anxiously after they exchanged dollars into British pounds. They proceeded through Customs rolling their suitcases. Luckily, they found their uniformed driver, identified by a sign saying WYN-TV, and warmly greeted him. Soon on their way, they would reach Oxford in just over an hour.

In the early morning sunlight, they arrived at their destination in the university town. They sleepily gazed at the lush green gardens and dreamy golden spires of the ancient university. They checked into an expensive hotel Biz liked. It was quiet and sedate. And the reception rooms were traditionally decorated with heavy carpets, silk drapes, and damask sofas.

After short naps, they met again in the lobby for lunch and a walk. Biz looked forward to seeing how the town had changed, and the others had not yet seen it. Having missed part of a night's sleep, she felt exhausted but did not show it or complain.

Oxford had a way of propelling Biz to action as few other places could. Simply being there energized her and made her troubles melt away. She had known every inch of it while taking classes. She remembered much time spent in pubs with friends and many of her favorite secret memories: sunny languid afternoons, parties in college gardens, nights of dancing. She had even seen royal limousines parked, perhaps when young royals attended graduation ceremonies. She appreciated the sights of ancient colleges as they shimmered in the silver mist, cobblestone streets such as the Turl, and libraries like the Bodleian. She could not resist shopping in good bookstores she found either. She might need novels to unwind on the European mainland, where finding them in English might be harder.

Despite her happy surroundings, Biz found herself on edge. She resolved to keep her eyes peeled for suspicious activity for a few more days. If nothing unusual happened by then, she would relax and hope she had only imagined being followed.

The next day, she met briefly with some of her interviewees at the business school on the railway side of town. At the internationally respected program, she interviewed Lord Dawson but did not take much of his time. After taking a few of her questions, he said he had to prepare for the upcoming meeting of finance ministers that she also planned to attend in Paris. She planned to interview him another time in Greece with more questions.

To spend time in his presence and learn more about his business, she probably would have taken the opportunity to visit his nearby estate had she been invited. Her goal, to interview a few British executives and talk to them about business and art, had been conceived for a special report on British business. She hoped they could also inform her more fully on recent art heists.

The team could not persuade their British hosts to take formal afternoon tea with them. And Lord Dawson, with his oversized ego and sense of entitlement, still bothered her personally although she kept it quiet. He was not one of her favorites. Somehow, the tension and vibrations he radiated made her fear and suspect him, she knew not why. She heard he intimidated most people. She secretly dreaded interviewing him again in Athens, not that she desired to have much of his time.

She walked alone across the busy wide road to the Ashmolean Museum to enjoy her favorite paintings for a few minutes. Luckily, the weather in Oxford remained mostly sunny and did not present the relentless rain for which England had become known. Her sense of being watched was subsiding and ebbing like the tides surrounding the British Isles, and she persuaded herself she had just imagined it.

Chapter 19

TOWARD THE END of the Oxford visit, Biz met the team's new temporary driver Stewart, Lord Dawson's driver, and he drove them around town. She vaguely remembered him from the New York insider trader interview when he said he had seen her. He personally took an interest in her stopover, looked out for her, and answered her questions.

"Have you always lived in England?" she asked him once.

Stewart looked at her in surprise. "I lived in New Jersey briefly years ago. Now I like meeting young Americans on scholarship here. I've been too busy to move back."

"Do you go into London often?" she asked him.

"Yes, I regularly drive his lordship to his enormous white townhouse in Grosvenor Square," he said seriously.

He extended an invitation to her alone at one point to attend dinner with him the following evening in London. As she considered it, she politely talked about her plans and how much she enjoyed visiting England. She finally replied the group planned to head into London for a couple of days before continuing on to France.

"Of course, if you came along with us it would be better if you could recommend a good restaurant where we could all go," she said, remembering their schedule.

He looked vaguely disappointed. "I can certainly drive your group into London. There is one fine restaurant called Roots but a reservation is almost impossible to obtain on short notice. Only a rock star could get a table there now but I'll see what I can do. It's good you're traveling expenses-paid, but I'm not. I've always wanted to eat there but, unfortunately, I have a previous commitment the same evening and can't have a really long dinner."

The same evening, the team agreed instantly when he told them he could drive them to London the next day in a large van. Incredibly, he also scored a coveted reservation at the popular restaurant. He must have been well-connected.

The traffic in the outer boroughs of London made the trip take well over an hour. On the way, they talked about tourist attractions.

"Have you ever been up the Eye?" he asked.

"No, but maybe we will tomorrow morning. Have you?"

"I hear it's great!" he said. "If you don't mind heights the way I do."

"We were thinking about it. Sounds like a good place to have on our itinerary," Biz said and the others agreed. They were looking forward to it.

They were quickly approaching Central

London. She turned around to have a conversation with Stewart. His arm accidentally brushed hers, and her watch dropped out of sight between them as she sat in the front seat. They did not remark on it as he distracted them all with his humor and personal opinions. Almost immediately, they reached the hotel.

"Thank you for taking time out to reserve the dinner. It's unfortunate you can't stay." She had a lot on her mind, and forgot about the watch.

"My pleasure and I hope you'll have many more of them in *la belle France*," he said. "I'll contact you, I promise."

After he deposited their equipment and suitcases on the sidewalk of their hotel in Mayfair, he leaned over to wave. On his wrist a silvery-gold bracelet with a gold monogram glinted in the sun.

Biz noticed the bright flash of his incongruous jewelry as she shook his hand in farewell and briefly wondered why he sounded so sure they would meet again.

"Goodbye," she said. "And I hope it's sunny again *if* we meet in the future."

Chapter 20

STEWART LIVED a quiet simple life in England. His room near Oxford, the center of learning located in the heart of the English countryside, had been a lucky find. He rented a single furnished room with two tall arched Gothic windows, and an antique Jacobean chest instead of a closet.

Yet he was discontented, and in time became ever more vengeful. In his bed-sitter, he had the use of a kitchen and shared the bath. While uncrowded, he did not have as much space as he would have liked, and had been accustomed to having, and found the other tenants complicated his life. He did not invite anyone else inside his room or listen to loud music. The town provided him with plenty of street noise through his thin windows.

The Diamondbacks kept extracting money from him to pay his debts and left him little to spend. Since the Diamondbacks freed him from jail before a judge sent him to prison, he owed them his life and found himself at the bottom rung of the Diamondbacks ladder. He had to obey them and work within the hierarchy. And any time Vince thought he could resign from his job with the syndicate, they did something that made him more dependent on them.

Indeed, the Diamondbacks had saved him. Considered at small risk of escaping, he stayed in a small county jail. His cell had been secured with only a single padlock, and was easily cracked open by the Diamondbacks using a sledgehammer. They stormed his cell without getting caught, and hustled him into a van. They also fitted him with a false beard and mustache as a disguise. They escaped by boat and gave him a ride all the way to Boston.

His conspirators made it appear as if his boat had been deserted. They left signs with the DB logo crest of the Diamondbacks on the empty boat, and passengers were presumed to have drowned. The Diamondbacks came through for him, gave him a passport in Boston, and sent him on his way to England on a private jet.

When Vinnie arrived in England, he walked around and watched the people in the airport and on the streets. He vowed revenge on those who had accused him and punishment for those who wanted to put him away. He adopted a new Anglo name, and had to be grateful not to be imprisoned for a long time back in America.

At night, after he fell asleep in front of his television or computer screen he usually slept fitfully, worrying about the next day's tasks. His days left him restless and unhappy. He had little to comfort him but his memories. He would make Biz pay for this, of that he was sure.

Chapter 21

IN THE MORNING haze when the mind has yet to completely awaken, one can hope for a day overflowing with possibilities. In London, Arthur liked to wake up to colors and designs he might choose to paint during the day. He thought of the day ahead as he yawned, gazing at Tower Bridge through his clean floor-to-ceiling windows. The weather in London that November morning inspired outdoor exercise. With a slight headache, he dressed in his running gear, and listened to his radio about the theft of a Picasso from a London museum. He would have to check that out later.

First, he needed to take a quick run. How predictable his life had become, he thought. Yet the comfort he drew from that same predictability urged him to awaken and make plans. To really wake up, he would head to the Thames with the goal of improving his personal best thirty-five-minute record. He had grown well-aware of the benefits of exercise, despite the precious moments it subtracted from his day.

Mostly Arthur enjoyed a rather solitary life. A little too solitary, he fretted to himself, as he thought of Sarah. Lady Sarah. Their parents had both belonged to the Chaucerian Club and he had thrown her a half-birthday party the previous spring. Unfortunately, the party had not pleased her. In fact, she had not liked being reminded of her birthday at all. She had been very bossy, and complained she had not been invited to be involved with the decorations, and would have handled everything differently. It was always something like this with Lady Sarah.

Arthur knew he needed to meet more women, but was interested in being known first and foremost as a disciplined knowledgeable artist and art historian.

He admittedly liked to flirt and did so at every opportunity. He dreaded hearing from any one of his previous girlfriends. A phone call someday might tell him about children he helped conceive without being aware of it. He had certainly attempted to settle down and commit to Lady Sarah. And that hadn't made him happy either.

When he wanted to talk and meet people he could go to the fairly distant Chaucerian Club. This elite club to which his parents had belonged had recently changed to a new address, having bought a building owned by his family. He would have had to reacquaint himself with his Range Rover to get there. Instead, he usually headed to the King's Arms Pub around the corner to have a few pints and crack jokes with the bartender. He was also an owner of the building as an added incentive.

This morning Arthur warmed up with stretching exercises and arm weights for twenty minutes. He took the elevator to the main floor and without losing any time crossed the road to the wide sidewalk overlooking the river on the other side of the roadway.

He started his run along the familiar route, passed a statue by the river and gradually picked up his speed as the walkway ahead of him lengthened. The sun looked as if it would make a long golden arc into the sky and shine boldly through a beautiful tableau of cirrus clouds promising a day full of sunshine. His American visitors at the gallery would like that.

Arthur intended to buy supplies at his favorite art store the same morning after his run. After that, he would call contacts to learn more about the Picasso heist and spend time at the Newland Gallery. He looked forward to meeting his American visitors yet had mixed feelings, too, not being the greatest fan of their country.

He had just finished a painting of a woman he had long dreamed of meeting with golden shoulder-length hair. He decided if he ever did find her in real life, he would take it as a sign that she was the one for him.

Arthur had long been left to his own ingenuity to create his own career path. His parents had died fifteen years earlier on a ski trip to the Austrian Alps. The money he received from his parents' will was more than enough to buy his comfortable flat in the city after his graduation from the University of Oxford. Of course, it could not make up for not having them around.

He knew he could have company more often if he wanted, and except for occasional aching pangs of loneliness from time to time, considered his life comfortable. He did sometimes grow worried this might be all there would be to his life. He certainly did not want to grow old alone and did not fancy the idea of living alone forever.

Four runners jogged along the path ahead of him. The first two were a pair of women, one with bright blond hair in a ponytail. Another man and woman jogged slightly ahead of them. Around him, he could see dogs being walked and couples holding hands. Funny, couples tended to walk in the late afternoon or evening more than in the morning especially this early. He fantasized how great it would be to take an early morning walk with someone he loved. Sarah had always preferred her beauty sleep to the jarring prospect of early morning runs.

For some reason, Arthur focused on the woman with her hair in a ponytail. She wore a red windbreaker and was clearly well-groomed even from a distance. She had a pretty appearance, and reminded him of Biz whom he expected to meet later that day. Her gait appeared precise and measured. He had always admired exactly this gait in a jogger though he felt sure he did not have it himself.

"Good morning," he said. Sleek and sure-footed, he rapidly gained on the group and was about to advance and pass them at high speed.

The woman turned to look at him, and in the same fleeting moment, her foot lodged in a large crack in the sidewalk. She fell and almost sprained her ankle. Shrieking in pain, she called out to the couple ahead to stop.

Arthur looked back at the startled jogger. With surprise, he noticed the woman in the red windbreaker actually was Biz Andrews.

"I'm so sorry if I distracted you. Please let me give you a hand," he insisted.

"I feel faint. I think I twisted my ankle. I hope I haven't sprained it. Would you mind helping me sit on the bench?"

Without hesitation Arthur lifted her slim figure to a bench where she could sit more comfortably, and helped examine and massage her ankle. His brief disappointment at the possible loss of a new record instantly disappeared.

"Thank you very much. It's sore but I don't think it's been hurt too much," Biz said.

Her cameraman Landon sighed guiltily in relief and admitted, "Good to hear. We have a busy schedule ahead of us in France and Italy. Spraining an ankle would definitely hurt our plans."

"That's completely my fault. Never a good idea to distract a focused runner," Arthur said sheepishly.

Biz looked up again at Arthur and smiled at the chiding, despite the pain. "I'm fine, Arthur, thank you. Not your fault. We're looking forward to seeing your gallery show late morning when we're finished our other plans."

Arthur saw that Biz's people were taking care of her, so he nodded in salute and took off to finish his run very much looking forward to the coming day's possibilities.

Chapter 22

THE TEAM TAXIED to the London Eye that morning, in deference to Biz's tender ankle. She did not want to walk far. After they entered through sliding glass doors of the attraction, a giant circular windowed pod lifted and carried them over the top, to stunning views. The slow ride offered incredible vistas of the Houses of Parliament and the City of London spreading to the horizon. Amazing photos recorded the highlights of their trip.

They took in the market at nearby Covent Garden, and then headed to the Newland Gallery. As they entered through the unique carved teak door of the Gallery, Biz and Arthur greeted each other with wide smiles. Despite, or perhaps because of all the miles she had traveled, she felt relieved their meeting had worked out.

"How's your ankle? Have you recovered?" He gazed at her sympathetically. His friendly expression instantly charmed her again.

He, in turn, remembered how attracted he had been to Biz at their first meeting, and felt magnetized to her again. Her dress flattered her terrific figure and defined her shoulders and arms to advantage. Her shapely legs, despite a slight limp, signaled major devotion to vigorous exercise. He wondered if she jogged often, and bit his lip before he asked.

"Thank you very much for lifting and carrying me the way you did this morning. I really appreciate that. I did almost take a bad tumble out there but I'm mostly better now. I do have to thank you."

"Are you here long?" he asked.

"I'm afraid not, just a few hours. We're off to France this evening," she said.

"I hope you've enjoyed your trip to England," he said with quiet warmth and sincerity. "I wanted to speak to you again after your party. I didn't thank you enough and tell you how much I enjoyed it."

"You're welcome, Arthur. We're having a spectacular day here. It isn't often we can see to the top of the world as we did today in the London Eye," she added to flatter him on his city.

The Americans wandered around the gallery and remarked quietly among themselves on the pictures. It seemed to Arthur his detailed oils especially captured Biz's interest. After giving her fifteen minutes to walk around, he approached her again.

"Do you like them?"

"Like them? I love them." said Biz. "I'd prefer to buy the large one but it would have to be sent a long way."

She was referring to his painting of a woman wearing a long dress and holding a parasol. His paintings were so oversized, most people assumed they were more expensive than they actually were. He had a few smaller ones but usually he liked to fill a huge canvas with his typically ambitious displays.

"Would you like it delivered to the United States?" he asked.

"New Jersey," she confirmed matter-of-factly. "But perhaps I should think about one of your smaller pieces."

He led her over to a canvas with richly-hued violets, blues, and greens in his painstakingly detailed delicate Impressionist style. He preferred to represent the real world of the urban and the rural. And there were even abstract paintings, large canvases filled with bright splashes of red, black, yellow, and white.

An unexpected thought struck him speechless. As he gazed at her, time locked itself as a fixed element. In some strange way, she resembled the girl in the canvas he was working on. She was the beautiful woman he had been painting for months, the one who inhabited his secret dreams. Her lips resembled pink rosebuds. Her hair shone. Finally, he had found the woman he had painted.

He felt the room shake rather like a tremor. His heart beat alarmingly rapidly and he felt light-headed. His balance became unstable and he almost blacked out.

He excused himself as he walked toward the open front door and sat down, briefly closing his eyes. It had happened so unexpectedly. He tried to imagine, with sinking anxiety, any way he could possibly prolong her one and only visit to the gallery. He did not want to let her slip away. He had heard some people say they were so desperate in their search for true love, they consulted psychotherapists. He did not intend to be one of them, and forced himself to snap out of this mood.

By the time he opened his eyes, Biz stood directly in front of his chair expressing concern. Her style of beauty appeared almost old-fashioned in the sun. The warmth of the midday sun and the hum of the street traffic sent a series of shivers up his spine. How could that be? He stood up.

"Are you all right?" she asked.

Arthur, who prided himself on always being cool, was tongue-tied. He watched her and did not speak for a matter of minutes.

"Is something the matter?" she continued.

Arthur did not say anything. He could not, for some reason. His dry mouth was clamped shut with unaccustomed anxiety and fear of losing her. Exactly when he should have spoken to her, he was struck speechless.

Clearly misreading his actions, she said, "If you think it's too much trouble, you could have it delivered to our hotel here in London. Maybe they would send it on. I do think I would prefer to buy the large painting, if it's available."

Reluctantly, he motioned to a redheaded saleswoman, patiently waiting in a corner, to take over for him and finish the sale. He could do little else but smile weakly at Biz and her friends.

If he were ever going to act, he had to right now. Else it might be the last time he might see her. If only he could show her the canvas of the almost-finished painting.

As the woman of his dreams paid the clerk, Arthur had an idea. He approached Biz, finally knowing what to say.

"We should talk about art thefts. And as it happens, I have another painting I think you might be interested in. It's a painting of a lady who resembles you more than a little," he said politely. "Perhaps I could show it to you? Would you like to see it?"

She gazed at him in surprise, not for the first time, he suspected. Nor the last, he hoped.

"Yes, we haven't much time, but it's true we were going to discuss art thefts," she said smoothly.

He handed her a card with his address on it. "My flat is only a few minutes away."

She checked with the others and they all agreed to follow her lead and see the painting with her.

As the team from WYN-TV silently entered Arthur's home an hour later, Biz gasped in surprise. Of course, there was nothing at all flat about it or the incredibly exciting views of the city. The River Thames could be seen from almost every window. She marveled that an artist could afford such extravagant space in the center of London.

Arthur's stunning loft in the eastern side of London had been built almost entirely of impressive glass windows, shining marble floors, and gleaming mahogany cabinets. Besides having one spacious bedroom, kitchen, and living room, he had a tall garden room with plenty of natural sunlight converted into an artist's studio. The unusual, light-filled conservatory with a glass roof and doors extended to a large party deck with a wide view of the river. It was everything he needed and proved ideal for painting and growing plants and vines.

Arthur told them he fundamentally needed a

lot of space to paint. His well-designed studio helped him concentrate and increased his output. He credited sound-proofing efforts on the windows, floors, and walls for keeping the sounds of London at bay. They had commanded a premium price to install but were worth every penny.

Then Biz saw the painting. She gazed at it, clearly astonished to behold the uncanny resemblance of the woman's face in the painting to her own.

"It's epic. I would love to have it," she said immediately. "It's almost as if you made this painting expecting me to show up and buy it."

"It's certainly a large painting. But I'm not sure it would arrive by boat in time for your holidays," he said carefully.

"I'd like it anyway, whenever it comes."

"Then it's yours," he said, feeling almost giddy.

She seemed to sense the intensity in the air and was aware they had spectators. "Perhaps we could have our art theft discussion with a cup of tea. Do you know anywhere close?" she asked him gently.

"I happen to own just the place," he said.

The group wandered into a small eating establishment identified by a quaint blue wooden sign over a light blue-and-white striped awning. The divine tea room, daringly named The Devonshire Poacher, smelled refreshing and sweet, rather like a bakery. The thoughtfully decorated room they entered had a bright airy atmosphere with striped window curtains and tablecloths on a white marble floor.

Biz sat beside Arthur at the corner of a marble-top table and waited to be served a fresh pot of tea and a mouthwatering assortment of fresh pastries. Her friends sat at a separate table. They said they were planning to shop for mementos as soon as they were finished and could get away. But Arthur could tell they were also trying to give him and Biz some space, while still keeping an eye on her.

She appeared extraordinarily beautiful as she relaxed in the sunlight. It made him want to learn more about her, to say the least.

"Biz is an interesting name. What's it short for?"

"Elizabeth," she said. "My parents used to prefer to call me Eliza until I chose Biz as a teenager."

He nodded to the adjacent table. "Your friends are doing a good job of keeping their eyes trained on you."

She turned to her coworkers with a quizzical smile. "They're with me all the time when we travel abroad. Since I'm on television in America, most people recognize me. Just need to be extra careful. Of course, I don't usually get recognized when I travel abroad."

Their tea arrived with delicate squares of sandwich and luscious cakes. Biz checked the strength and quality of the tea in a silver pot and poured it into their cups. It was still too hot to drink.

"Cheers to privacy. And to refreshing interludes," he said. "And to Omega-3s," he added as they waited for their tea to cool. He helped himself to light, savory salmon sandwiches.

She nodded and delicately chose a celery sandwich as well. "Have you heard anything more about the Picasso theft?"

"Yes, back to business. According to my sources the thieves stole only one painting. They left the checkered sign of the Diamondbacks at the scene. Over time, I should hear further details on how it was done."

"That's major," she said. "Is there anything else? Did you hear anymore details?"

"That's all I've heard so far. But I wanted to tell you sooner rather than later that it was probably the Diamondbacks."

"Thank you for that. Please let me know as you learn more."

"Naturally," he replied.

She sipped her hot tea cautiously. After a pause, she asked, "Have you always loved art?"

"My grandparents had art in the castle where they lived and which they inherited. I used to marvel at the paintings they had kept in the family for many years, the length of time they had taken to create and the labors of love they were for the artists. I learned to appreciate the structure of lines in a fine piece. I couldn't duplicate the styles painted in portraits of my ancestors and no one could teach me so I created my own signature style."

"Fascinating, thank you."

Sparkles of attraction definitely crackled between them. He liked what he saw of her. He enjoyed watching her pick up her cup and set it down on her saucer over and over again. And he unknowingly comforted her as he sipped his milk-flavored Earl Grey.

With her blessing, and friendly salutes, Jessie and Gina got up and left the tea shop to walk around the nearby market district. Landon went back to the hotel to pick up their suitcases leaving Biz and

Arthur alone.

"I have a personal question," she said. "I'm just curious and you don't have to answer if you don't want to, but which schools did you attend?"

As his voice peeled with laughter, he turned to her confidentially. "Usually I don't talk about it because it makes me feel boastful. Actually, hardly anyone bothers to ask anymore. I went to good schools: Eton, and Balliol College at Oxford. After university my hobby for painting became my obsession and then turned into my career." Their eyes locked. "I find you easy to talk to and that's very unusual for me." Biz beamed and Arthur smiled back at her as he ate a fresh scone laden with strawberry jam and dripped some clotted cream. "You must be well-suited to journalism since you like to travel. And you're good at getting people to talk."

"You'd be surprised how hard it used to be for me to trust people unless I've known them for a long time," Biz said. Then she paused. "Have you ever thought how happy you are to have met someone and how disastrous it would have been for your life if you hadn't? Sometimes it's like a miracle."

They talked about the art world and their interests. The hours sped by all too quickly. Who would have thought so much excitement and business could happen with tea, sandwiches, and cakes in the afternoon, they marveled. They had stayed two hours, far longer than the more usual half-hour tea service. Apart from a manager, Arthur went mostly unrecognized as the landlord. The tea shop had long since stopped serving and had posted a 'closed' sign on the door. The wait staffs hovered keen to finish working for the day.

Biz and the team had a plane to catch. She had missed souvenir shopping, not that she minded a bit. Jessie and Gina had come back happily laden and were standing outside, growing extremely anxious to head to Heathrow Airport. As the others waited at the hired car, they busily repacked and folded their purchases into bulging suitcases that Landon had retrieved from the hotel.

Biz and Arthur suddenly had to bid each other a hasty farewell.

"I'm sorry I have to go," she said.

"Thanks for your time. When I visit the States again I'll be sure to look you up," Arthur promised.

"You have my email address. I'll look forward to receiving your paintings."

She shook his hand and turned toward the waiting car. Then as if on impulse, she turned around, rushed back to him, and surprised him with a quick peck on the cheek.

He held her kindly, and gave her a longer kiss. "Goodbye," he said sadly.

Chapter 23

LANDON NOTICED THAT Biz sat quietly subdued. The limousine advanced at high speed through teeming London crowds on the way to the airport. As they passed a huge and popular stone castle, and avoided colliding with other vehicles and surging tourists, he took it upon himself to speak and distract her.

"That's the Tower of London in which Mary, Queen of Scots was imprisoned and Lady Jane Grey was beheaded. The Crown Jewels are on view in that building. If we had time we could see them."

Around the solid square crenellated structure with turrets, red-costumed security guards, known as Beefeaters, stood sentry. The enormous fortress had been built long before for earlier, purely historical, security reasons, and had known a tumultuous existence if its size was any indication.

They were all tired and grew quiet, knowing they had many more days to spend in one another's company before the end of the trip. Although they cooperated well, they had begun to wear on each other's nerves because of their mutual reliance and the intensity of the journey.

"We don't have time for it so what's your point?" asked Biz.

"Just saying," said Landon and turned to read his guide.

"I'm sorry." Biz sighed. "That was unkind. I didn't mean it."

In the ensuing silence, Biz gazed wistfully through the window on the bumpy ride at jostling crowds, and wished she had allowed more time in her tight schedule to spend in London with Arthur. She thought sadly how each mile they drove placed another one between them, and noticed herself connecting the dots between finding a mate and thinking of Arthur. People pulled at her heart strings more than places, she had always found.

She checked her left wrist to check the hour as the car headed to the airport for the short flight to Paris but found she was not wearing her timepiece and could not find it in her crocodile handbag. She was proud of her rose gold watch with tiny diamonds and had bought it for herself.

Gina and Jessie gazed at her sympathetically.

"I couldn't have lost it. I'm phoning the hotel to see if they have it," she said.

A few minutes later she turned off the phone, upset, almost in tears. "The hotel doesn't have it."

"You haven't been wearing it all day," said Gina.

She realized Gina was right. The thought occurred to her she had taken it off briefly the previous day to make another slight time change. She had been with Stewart in his van driving to London.

She felt ashamed to even think of asking such a trustworthy driver as Stewart if he had seen it. They did not have an easy way of contacting each other, and she hoped he kept it if he found it, and might contact them. Her coworkers had been in and out of her hotel room briefly the same morning, but she trusted them completely. She worried she would have to surrender the idea of finding it again, and felt vulnerable and angry at the same time.

Chapter 24

RICHARD ANDREWS had been reviewing court decisions and procedural law at Warm Springs Farms. Ensconced in his green leather chair, he sat comfortably at his carved mahogany desk. His masculine book-lined study, decorated with emerald velvet curtains was lit by solid brass lamps with deep green shades. At home for a light lunch, he smiled as he answered his phone and welcomed the voice of his daughter.

"I hope you've had a pleasant time so far," he said.

"As always, England hopelessly charms me," Biz admitted. "We're driving on our way to Heathrow Airport. The itinerary ahead of us is still Paris and Rome. I'm glad I don't have to travel around and navigate by myself. We're in a limousine together now."

"I saw your report from Oxford. Good work as always." He was enjoying the break from work.

"Thanks. How're you and Mom?" She added sounding wistful. "I miss you."

"We miss you, too. We went into the city last night to attend a symphony concert at Rockefeller University. Your mother's back is bothering her again and I have a little arthritis in my foot. Otherwise, we're fine. We're about to take an impromptu vacation in the Caribbean. If you have time you could come with us."

"Where are you going this time?"

"We thought we'd try St. John instead of Barbados again, just for a long weekend. Same place as last time. Just wanted to ask if there's any chance you could come with us after you get back?"

"Thanks for asking. It sounds wonderful but I'm too busy now between this trip and my tight schedule. I can't plan ahead much these days for holidays. Just remember to bring some of your attorney novels to read on the beach," she ribbed him.

"Wouldn't dream of forgetting." Then he added, "We'll be glad when you're back on American soil."

"Thanks again. I hope you have a good time and I'm glad to hear you're healthy," she said. "Look, Dad, I called because my watch, my good watch, has disappeared."

"I'm sorry to hear that," Richard replied. "Wait, here's your mother. She wants to speak with you."

Joan hurried to take the phone he held out to her and asked after her health. She had just been shopping at the Mall at Short Hills following a meeting of the Harding Garden Club. In flower-arranging circles, she had become well-known as an ikebana expert. She had published a coffee table picture book on the topic and had just given a talk.

"I hope you're all right," Joan said. Her high-treble voice softened.

"I'm okay. But my watch disappeared and it's making me miserable, among other things. Talking to you and Dad always cheers me up. That's why I called."

Her mother sounded a note of concern. "That's terrible about your watch. I'm sorry to hear that. I hope it shows up in your luggage. And I'm glad you called. Do you remember you thought a man might have followed you and sat in a car at the end of the driveway?"

"Absolutely, I'm still wondering about that."

"Today I spoke to our new neighbors. They recently moved into the farm next to us and they noticed him parked at the end of their driveway a couple of times. That makes me a little worried. Does your job require you to have a high level of security protection?"

Biz felt her throat catch. The idea that a security company might be lurking on her parents' driveway, possibly tailing her or them made her more angry than worried. The least the station could have done was warn her.

"Not as far as I know. I'll check into it. And don't worry, I'll be fine," she said sounding more convinced than she actually felt. "I'll be home again soon. Have fun on your trip and thanks for your concern. It means a lot."

Joan put down the phone after bidding her daughter goodbye. She turned to speak to Richard across the room.

"Rather odd, all this bad luck happening to Biz. Her planner stolen, the man in his car, and her watch missing. I hope some crazy person isn't after her."

Maybe good parenting never ends. Even after all these years, Joan had not stopped mothering, even after raising Biz and her brother through college and beyond. She constantly worried they might sink into unpredictably dangerous situations. Perhaps, her over-active imagination was aided by gruesome details from some of her husband's more sordid legal cases.

"That's very unlikely, I would think," Richard said. "I mean, why would anyone want to do that? She's on the financial newsbeat."

"It just makes me nervous," said Joan.

For a little while longer, they kissed on the sofa in his home office. He walked toward his car to drive to work, and she watched him out the window.

Sunlight peeked through silver-edged clouds and white pines rippled in the breeze. A recent light snow had gently dusted the grass with a possible nor'easter forecasted.

Chapter 25

AT HEATHROW AIRPORT again, the team awaited their turn to board a flight to Paris. Feeling excited, Biz decided she would not let an unfortunate loss cloud her generally positive memory of the trip so far. She liked England and always found British people so sensible and kind. She even liked their generally cool weather throughout the year. The wind and rain could be fairly severe at times, but mercifully thunder and lightning rarely occurred in Southern England.

Announcements came over the loudspeakers that their flight was delayed, and Biz decided to focus on the news. She was grateful to see persistent news updates on the television screen overhead about the art theft of the Picasso the previous night. The gallery where the theft had occurred had been left a sign with the Diamondbacks symbol. It would hit the art community hard given that Picasso paintings were especially highly regarded and among the most expensive. If the dreaded Diamondbacks were involved, similar thefts might happen again. Somehow, the thieves had to be caught.

Almost immediately, another news flash appeared on the screen. A train had supposedly passed into the tunnel beneath the English Channel, derailed, and burst into flames. Watching the disaster videos unfold in horrified shock, they worried the train explosion might in some way be connected to their delay.

Finally, after the long wait, Biz and her weary group were called to board the midsize jet for the flight to Paris. They expected to snooze and rest on the short flight. But the plane taxied out to the runway and, to the surprise of everyone, the engines ceased without any warning. Interior lights flickered and failed, and passengers twisted and turned anxiously. Flight attendants walked up and down the aisles trying to keep everyone calm. For the time being, the plane was not going anywhere.

Biz did not have any difficulty sitting in one place for any length of time and did not feel particularly bothered by claustrophobia. Calmly comforting herself, she placed her missing beloved timepiece in a pretty box in her imagination, and tied it with a bow that she had every intention of opening later.

Despite the power outage, she still had the use of her cell phone and decided to text Arthur. To her surprise, he texted her back immediately with a kind supportive message that this delay would pass.

If a man truly liked her, he would not make her wait long to hear back, she remembered. Ironically, Dean had once passed along this pearl of wisdom.

Biz found herself thinking about her parents and about the mysterious subcompact that had shown up near their house when she visited. If she was being watched, she chose to believe the station wanted to assess whether they could give her a higher clearance of level. To ascertain how trustworthy she might be, Biz found herself wildly speculating in what others ways the company might have already secretly tracked her. At the same time, she felt instinctively the television station had always been straightforward with her. Surely they would not do something like this without warning her.

What if they had been following her? Did that mean they knew about her and Mitch? She had always kept her affair and the miscarriage with Mitch secret, and worried off and on that it could jeopardize her job security and her savings, if anyone found out and threatened her. Their previous relationship would embarrass both of them if it went public and she had promised to keep it a secret.

Chapter 26

MITCH MORRIS initially noticed Biz when she worked for the company as a high school senior. He predicted her star power correctly after photos and videos of her proved extremely photogenic. After Columbia University accepted her, she continued to hold a series of summer jobs at the company.

He personally invited her to visit his family's summer place for company picnics. Toward the end of her junior year at Columbia, he called her into his corner office. As they looked out the huge windows overlooking Morris County that summer day, he said he only wanted to ask her what she planned to do after graduation.

She laughed at his easy question in uncomfortable relief, slightly intimidated by the entire room, the thick padded carpeting, the sight of his large desk decked out with several computers and televisions lining the wall. She replied that she was unsure of her future employment. She later considered her reaction inappropriate in the unexpected interview, embarrassed to laugh as she had in formal conversation. She assumed she had probably not landed the job.

Yet despite her pessimism she had been hired, and after joining WYN-TV full time, quickly worked her way to announcing a short news summary on air at midday. Her pieces played live, if not at prime time.

She grew to enjoy her career, and felt she had achieved a measure of success when she saw her name added to the elite list of anchors with limousine privileges. Not having to worry about transportation issues or changing companies led her take on more evening and weekend hours, and in turn helped increase her public popularity.

After a couple of years Mitch asked her out one day for lunch after her report, ostensibly to talk about work. He took her to her favorite restaurant, the best in the area, across the mighty Delaware River from Lambertville.

Lambertville, a western New Jersey town, had been named after the Lamberts. Located on the Delaware River, the town held a fish festival every spring and attracted crowds of New York, New Jersey, and Pennsylvania day-trippers to its art and antique shops and restaurants. In peaceful weather, the bustling borough appeared magical at all times of day from rosy-hued dawns to coppery-golden sunsets.

Biz generally preferred the light of the mornings, the most pristine time, with the day ahead beckoning joyfully and bursting with promise. She especially enjoyed driving into the small town where she could park easily and shop at any time.

They were seated at the best table in the picturesque restaurant with its scenic view, directly over the current of the river. A vigorous little stream nearby cascaded rapidly into the mightier Delaware, and sparkled silvery in the sunshine. Biz anxiously picked at her salad and gave him her most winning smile. What had she done to deserve this splendid treatment from the owner of the company?

Mitch chose a full-bodied wine from Australia to drink with the meal.

"Would you ever like to visit Australia?" he asked. It was only an innocent question, after he read the label on the bottle.

She was in awe of his wealth and unsure of his intent. Possibly due to her youthful twenty-five years, she misunderstood the source of his question.

"Are you asking if I've been there?"

She was unsure if he meant there might actually be a story to do there, or if he planned to expand the office and might want her to move there, or what. She passed on the wine and wondered why he asked about Australia.

Just to say something after he paused, she rather innocently continued, "It's certainly somewhere I'd like to visit some day but I'm happy here. New Jersey is my home and always has been."

"Where did you go on vacations with your parents when you were growing up?" he asked.

"Usually we'd go to Canada. My mother's from Ottawa, and her family gathered every summer for a few weeks near Ottawa in the hills outside at a lake they own there. It's a family compound, and it's been in the family since the area became popular with summer residents. They can all gather at once to relax for holidays. We swam a lot."

"Must have been fun. Where else did your family visit?"

"We also often flew to the Caribbean in the winter or spring, mostly Barbados, and sometimes we'd go on cruises in the Mediterranean or travel around Europe for a shorter time in the summer."

She idly speculated as to why he was so interested. Then she decided to relax. He had driven her, and he would drive her back to the office. He controlled her time in his role at the head of the company. If he wanted her to talk about her childhood vacations, she would comply happily.

Mitch sat back, swished his wine, and spilled it. "They were well off," he mused.

"They did all right. Mostly they took care of their land here in New Jersey. It's too much for them alone and they always needed gardeners to help them. I used to love to climb our trees. I'd take a book and spend hours just daydreaming."

Suddenly it occurred to Biz that she could use this opportunity to impress her boss and not just idle on about her family. She turned to business rather abruptly.

"Do you think rich people are taxed enough?" she asked.

Mitch himself asked lots of questions by nature and enjoyed discussions like this when he had time. He would challenge someone with a different opinion while sticking to his own, and find out all sides of the story before making his own judgment, on issues of international significance.

"Personally I think I'm taxed too much," he answered with a wry grin, "and I get most irritated if employees in the company don't finish the jobs we pay them to do. The government should tax corporations and individuals living off inherited wealth with low taxes the same as everyone else, not more, not less. I have much to be grateful for. They should think conscientiously about what exactly they think is worth supporting with donations. Sometimes I'm skeptical of the generosity of others, perhaps especially the wealthy, to fund social services through donations. Everyone's attention gets whipped around to the most fashionable cause, local or faraway."

Biz liked his answer. She was about to ask another probing question, then somehow got the sense maybe she should just be cool under the circumstances. "So, where did you travel on holidays?" she asked with a grin.

"We summered in Nantucket, Massachusetts and wintered in La Jolla, California," he said "I've been taking my family away on long weekends with the jet, usually anywhere within a four hour radius. I enjoy taking the time even though I'm usually thinking about the future of the news business."

"Of course, you're a gifted businessman," she said boldly stroking his ego.

He paused and then continued smoothly, "I could use some help with a Word document this afternoon. My secretary is at a dental appointment. You probably know all about Windows."

Biz felt startled. "I suppose so."

Mitch apparently had such an enjoyable lunch, he invited her again. He told her about his other companies. He showed her his large office with a sofa and a closet. It even had a large bathroom with a shower. He could sleep there if he had to. He started to invite her there to chat almost every day.

One day, as she was about to leave his office he gave her a kiss—a surprisingly lingering kiss. He invited her to come back the next evening to watch a movie with him. And she found herself unable to turn him down in every way.

It became the thing they did a couple times a week. He liked to loosen her tight clothes and stroke her breasts as they watched movies. One evening he pulled apart her legs and she opened herself up to him. He told her she was the most beautiful girl he had ever made love to and the most irresistible as he kissed her and gave her more pleasure than she had ever had with anyone else.

Ultimately, her plans twisted into an entirely new direction when she discovered he had made her pregnant. She was frightened, unable to confide even in her parents until she finally told her mother of her pregnancy and the identity of the baby's father. She did not have a plan; what she should do, how she would cope. She felt embarrassed, afraid, and unsure of her future.

The only certainty she knew was the father. When she told Mitch, he was cold, although he made it clear he felt sorry for her. He loved her but certainly not enough to leave his wife and help her raise a baby.

At the end of her sixth week, she had to keep to her bed with painful cramps and bleeding. She called her doctor in a panic. The office nurse told her it sounded as if she likely had a stillborn fetus and had better have a quick check up as an emergency in the hospital.

Ultimately, she lost the baby in a miscarriage. She was cleaned up with a procedure under total anesthesia after a spontaneous abortion ended the pregnancy in her nearby hospital. She took sick leave from work, and with her ever-understanding mother Joan, flew to a restful much-needed California vacation.

After that, she remained ever-conscious of the fact Mitch had not accepted any responsibility for a baby with her. If the baby had lived, her life would have changed. She could not contemplate the difference. She made a decision she would meet with Mitch and end her intimate relationship with him. It had all been a mistake from the start. She would simply have to turn away from him forever as a possible candidate for marriage, and hoped in time her pain would subside as her doctor had said it would. She scheduled a brief telephone conversation with Mitch at his office during which she asked if they could meet for dinner.

They met in a classic French restaurant in New York. She wore a tailored gray suit with a ruby necklace and bracelet and a white shirt. With Mitch wearing a pin-striped suit and shiny dress shoes, they looked all business.

As they dined on a five-course meal, Biz picked at her food. "I'm sorry if I inconvenienced you this evening," she said. "There are a few important things I want to speak to you about."

"Whatever I can do for you I will. You know that," he said kindly.

As Biz registered the hollowness in his words, sadness bubbled up. "I loved you," she said, "and I prefer to believe you loved me. Maybe you were correct and marriage might not have worked. We'll never know. I've been through an unexpected ordeal with this miscarriage and I blame myself for a nightmare that could have been avoided if we had taken better care."

Mitch remained silent as he offered his

undivided attention.

"I have to say I admire the station you've built," Biz continued, "and I really enjoy working there but somehow being at WYN-TV doesn't feel right anymore. It's become hard for me to concentrate on working anytime you come near me. I've been offered a position at another station, and I'm thinking of taking it."

As Mitch listened to her, he reached into his pocket. To her utter astonishment, he pulled out his wallet and proceeded to cut her a check.

"Here. Take it. I want to keep you at the company. Don't even think about going to one of our competitors."

He handed her the check, and smiled at her with compassion.

She managed to gasp, "This is a huge amount."

"Don't you want to take it?" he asked her.

As she watched him, he looked up. Their eyes locked and did not move away for several moments.

"You're sure you want to give this to me?" she said.

"It's all right," he said. "Don't worry, I can just move some money into this account. There's just one condition."

"What?"

"It must remain a secret."

"I see." She stared at the check.

"It secures both our futures," he said kindly and Biz suddenly understood that both of their reputations were potentially at stake.

"Thank you very much," she said simply.

So she was able to buy a house in her favorite town, find a nice place to live and try to put all this heartbreak behind her.

After a five hour wait, the lights and power came back on, and the plane finally taxied along the runway and took off. All the passengers applauded when it landed in Paris just over an hour later. Biz and her crew had never felt as relieved to leave an airplane. They could hardly wait to stretch their muscles, and were glad to have the flight behind them. They remembered to thank the crew members, and gratefully entered the busy airport concourse.

Chapter 27

THE MORNING AFTER they reached Paris, the group wandered around the city. They had stayed overnight at a newly renovated hotel across from the coffee shop Le Matin du Monde. After having numerous cups of café au lait, they had a drive past sights they would visit in person, if only they had more time. The Louvre and Musée d'Orsay appeared especially inviting and important from the outside. Biz dreamed of having the opportunity to spend the whole day in the art museums and watch a show at the Paris Opera House. The team had just agreed to have a bite to eat for lunch when her phone rang. To her surprise, it was Arthur.

"Turns out I decided to head into Paris after all late last evening," Arthur said and yawned. "I drove to the Channel tunnel worrying about a friend, only to find the incident had been inaccurately reported. The derailment and fire were actually outside the tunnel, and my friend had a minor unrelated car accident, so being a good way here already, I just kept going. I arrived in Paris this morning and slept a few hours at a hotel."

"You must have been driving quickly," she remarked.

"I didn't exactly waste time. And I'd very much like to see you again."

"We're about to have our lunch at one of my favorite restaurants near the Eiffel Tower. Would you like to meet us?"

It would be a huge relief for the team to have Arthur around.

Her thoughts drifted happily to seeing him again. She told the team she needed to learn more financial information from Arthur mostly about art to use for their reports.

They nodded and smiled, knowing better.

When Arthur arrived at the restaurant, the group welcomed him and talked about the sights they would visit if they had more time. By then, they had painstakingly examined the French menu and ordered drinks and so on. He quickly caught up with them and ordered a meal, although they had used the time waiting for him well enough.

They enjoyed the wine and appetizers carefully placed on their compact table. It was evident to Biz that Arthur was not only there for her. He wasted no time drawing the whole team near him and getting to the point.

"I investigated yesterday's act of terrorism at the Channel Tunnel and it made me think. Some consider me a world expert on art heists, as you may know, as much as anyone on the outside of them can be. But I can say with certainty the Diamondbacks are the most famous organized group in Europe. They're responsible for all levels of jewelry, art thefts, and assorted criminal activities. They make counterfeit passports and visas, and have organized gambling, prostitution, and other criminal activities all over Western and Eastern Europe. They recruit new members and organize them in small cells responsible to the larger syndicate. I'm currently learning more about the composition and location of the syndicate and its reach. You wouldn't want to cross them, let me warn you. They're very secretive and work hard to keep it that way."

They gazed at Arthur with fascinated interest.

"We're certainly aware of them," said Jessie, tapping her cowboy boots impatiently. "We have them on our radar and want to expose their activities to a wider audience in America. You should stay with us and help us get the word out, maybe root them out. Our mission is incredibly ambitious."

"I'd be happy to," said Arthur, "but again you should know what you'll be facing. These are professionals. They'll go to any length to get what they want and are very hard to trace. They're careful to escape fingerprint detection and even take powerful drugs to smooth their fingertips."

"My father told me about them," Biz said. "He prosecuted a case in which a member of the Diamondbacks escaped from jail in New Jersey."

"Yes, I remember that case. It was a great scandal at the time and embarrassing, no doubt. He was freed from jail just before the sentencing by other members of the gang. Except for the sign of the Diamondbacks that investigators found in the boat, he disappeared without trace."

A rare feeling of ease washed over Biz. She felt relieved they had a real expert to guide them and to strengthen the validity of her reports. When lunch was over, she invited him to take a short stroll with her the next morning.

At seven o'clock, Biz and Arthur met at her hotel, and found their way to the Seine. They stopped to gaze at the mighty Notre Dame Cathedral, stunning in scope and detail at any time of day. While at night the church shone like a Christmas tree, the early morning light glowed in a golden, luminescent haze around the incredibly impressive edifice. She basked in the panoramic view, standing at the banks of the river as the city awoke hushed quiet and lovely. She would not have missed it for the world.

Her ankle still gave her occasional pain but she was able to walk easily after taking a couple of pills for muscle pain. The couple sat in a coffee shop to discuss the day's schedule. Biz mentioned how she wished she had time for the Louvre or the Paris Opera House.

"You've never been inside the Paris Opera House? Well, we could see the visiting Danish Ballet this evening if you're interested."

With this, he took her breath away.

"I'd absolutely love to see the ballet." She turned away crestfallen and worried. "I'm sorry I just haven't any time to figure out how to buy tickets."

"Leave it to me. I'll purchase them and meet you outside the Opera House at the Galeries Lafayette this afternoon. We can shop first."

Arthur beamed happily as they said goodbye and she waved as she walked into the hotel dreamy eyed. What a dreamboat, she thought giddily.

Biz entered her own room at the hotel for a

few minutes. She carefully removed her shoes and sat on her chair to relax for a few minutes before meeting her associates. As she tried to mentally prepare for the day's interviews, her mind grew jumbled and she realized she felt uncomfortable. Was it hypocritical to value her independence so consistently yet crave romance at the same time?

Chapter 28

THE FINANCE MINISTERS in Paris held their meetings in an impressive pillared marble building, resplendent with historic significance. American reporters posed in front giving brief updated newscasts. Viewers liked to hear familiar voices and watch faces they recognized in reports from abroad.

Biz's role had become a hugely important responsibility but one she had gradually grown into. She managed to write her reports on time, despite the fact that the slowdown from London to Paris and the time she had spent with Arthur had thrown her drastically off schedule.

Jessie and Landon produced clearly defined reports. Landon photographed in video and beamed them to New York showing them in real time to television stations all over the United States. Jessie and Gina helped her with the scripts and listened to meetings. The financial news they gathered could actually move financial markets and had been known to influence monetary policy and investor sentiment so the facts had to be accurate and correct. It took all she could remember from economics courses and learned on the job to make sense of the pronouncements, often translated and mistranslated, of these finance ministers.

Feeling motivated to use every moment wisely, Biz finished her work quickly and caught a cab to meet Arthur. As they went shopping together, she considered her circumstances secretly ironic. She wanted to keep her viewers aware of finances and yet occasionally had trouble wielding discipline over her own. And what handbags she saw: more colors of dyed crocodile than she could ever dream of surprised her at half the regular prices. She splurged on several irresistible handbags and had them sent ahead home.

As for jewelry, she admired finely faceted rubies, sapphires, and emeralds straight from India rooted in silver and twenty-two carat gold. The golden setting sun that evening played up their natural beauty and sparkled on an incredible number of facets. She located a gorgeous matching multi-colored bracelet, lifted and twirled the jewels carefully in the sunshine. And she ultimately purchased a unique multi-colored gemstone necklace of blue, green, and purple amethyst, her birthstone for the month of February. She had been hoping to find one for some time and would wear it with an indigo satin blue shirtdress on television.

Arthur watched and appeared to scrutinize her as she admired them.

"Getting fancy ideas, I see," he said finally with a wide smile.

"These are so beautiful. Collecting gemstone jewelry is one of my favorite hobbies. They're like works of art. It's fun to learn more about them. I buy rocks just for myself from time to time. Diamonds may be a girl's best friend but gemstones could be a close second," she said smiling with enthusiasm as she tried them on and focused on her reflection in the elegant mirrors.

"My grandmother used to have tiaras and some diamond jewelry," he said.

"Tiaras?" she said with glee. "Women rarely wear tiaras anymore. I adore searching for vintage jewelry." She laughed. "It's great you aren't walking away." She knew how skittish of jewelry some men could be.

"No. Although I have to admit, I've never bought any jewelry myself. Do you base your purchase on beauty?"

"Oh, not only beauty, there's a lot to know. We can find out the locations and practices of mines they originated from and where they were carved and faceted. Every gem has travelled probably thousands of miles just to get here. In the same way, we could always learn more about how our foods were grown and cultivated, our clothes were sewn, and under what conditions our wooden furniture was carved."

"I can't talk much about jewelry," he said, "but these are beautiful. Perhaps I should research my grandmother's pieces. I'm enjoying looking at these with you actually. They're works of art as you said, and a fascinating study."

"I'd love to help you sort through her jewelry," she said. "I enjoy reading about gemstones and visiting international gem shows if only to learn more about them and add to my collections. It's definitely an area worth understanding. In some countries, the jewelry business exposes problems of exploitation and child labor. I did one special about gemstones but I could do another one in more depth. Maybe I should interview experts and question them about mining for gemstones and how minerals are mined for use in electronics and industry as well as jewelry. But that would involve traveling."

"I've been to Asia many times with my parents and I'd like to go back again," he said in an instant.

He pleased her in so many ways. As they walked around the Galeries, they shopped for clothes. She found he had simple tastes: blue jeans, nice crisp blue and white cotton shirts. He dressed for comfort before style but always appeared well-groomed. He was far from the stereotype of the disheveled artist.

When they entered the formidable edifice of the Paris Opera House later that evening, they left their shopping bags in the cloakroom. Arthur changed into black tie he found at the last minute, and Biz wore a beautiful new dress along with her new necklace. As she watched the ballet, she had a rare opportunity to reflect on the stunning design and feel of the opera house. Dancers pirouetted on stage in their lovely costumes. The action and the music transported her to a place of deep reflection on beauty and those blurry questions about what exactly she was striving for in her life.

Her mind wandered to the thought that she merely wanted the good life her fellow Americans aspired to have: world travel, fine hotels and restaurants, beautiful homes, furniture, apparel, electronics, jewelry, and well-built cars. She knew that if she sought happiness through material gains, she would always need an ever-increasing abundance of these to make her happy. At the same time, she found it difficult to counteract a rising flood of materialism.

And, of course, there was the search for love. She had grown conscious of a curious contradiction. Her desire to be married conflicted with her simultaneous resistance to giving up autonomy. But she liked Arthur. He was adorable. He had inspired her once again to review her life goals and think about whether she wanted to live alone forever, or even for the next ten or twenty years.

As they slowly headed to her hotel room, to which he accompanied her, she avoided glancing at him. She wanted to hold onto their relationship. But she would have to awaken early the next morning. He gazed at her intently as she thanked him politely for the lovely evening. He asked her out for lunch, waved good night, and walked back to the elevator.

She was able to meet him only once more in Paris, around midday, before heading to the airport that afternoon to travel to Italy, the team's next destination. On the sidewalk of a bistro, they ate delicious toasted sandwiches and drank chilled white wine. They had a leisurely walk in the district around the hotel, and she noticed her ankle felt better. Sadness intermittently pervaded her thoughts as fleeting as the rain shower that passed. Going away meant she would be apart from Arthur, and she worried it would be a long time before they could meet again.

"I guess we'll have to leave it open when we'll meet again. *When*, not *if*, I hope," Biz said sadly as she gazed at Arthur.

"I want us to meet again."

"Where there's a will, there's a way," she said

resolutely.

These were the last words they said to each other before they parted. Biz felt tears moistening her cheeks as she approached the team waiting for her. She could see her suitcase being stowed in the private airport van, and soon she had left the center of Paris.

Chapter 29

WHILE THE WEATHER in Paris had been cool, Italy promised warm sunny days, according to weather forecasts. As the jet engines at Charles De Gaulle Airport roared to life under a cloudy sky, the hearts of all the passengers in the aircraft unavoidably pounded in excitement, anticipating the short flight to Italy. The plane began to move and swiftly accelerated. The engines groaned louder and pulled the airliner along the ground at tremendous speed. It swiftly gained forward momentum, soared upward into the atmosphere, and quickly disappeared into the cloud layer and then above.

Despite already missing Arthur, Biz felt unmistakably exhilarated as she watched their progress out the window. For a few moments she could see rivers and the city nestled in the landscape below as the plane kept rising. As she sat, her private thoughts focused on the work the team hoped to accomplish in Italy. She wondered whether her news investigations could embarrass Italians. They often covered delicate areas where

Italian law intersected with the everyday standards of free speech expected in American journalism.

They arrived in Italy after an event-free flight, for which she felt blessed, and had a day to fill with research and reports before the finance meetings and scheduled interviews. She went to the Vatican vicinity with the crew and prepared a television report about an art theft from a bank. They had significant news that the Diamondbacks had left their insignia painted on a pillar. But that was all they left as evidence. Fingerprints were not found on any surfaces, making them harder to track.

Her thoughts continued to return back to Arthur. She wondered when she would see him again.

As if summoned, he sent her a text. The station had asked Arthur to fly to Rome to help further the investigation.

Her spirits soared as she read his news. With the continuing art thefts, she would need his ongoing advice.

The next day, Arthur flew into Rome's Fiumicino Airport and taxied to the Vatican to meet her and the crew busily filming the report she had prepared in Saint Peter's Square. They met as if they had been apart for years instead of hours. They were becoming quite fond of each other and did not care who else might be watching as they kissed each other in the bright sun that November morning. Even the sunlight appeared to bless them as it dazzled around them in a bright halo.

She said goodbye to her crew temporarily and excused herself, agreeing to meet them again later for drinks and dessert. She and Arthur walked for hours around the Vatican and through the Sistine

Chapel. Not the first visit for either, the Vatican Museums appeared enormous and impressed them anew. The exquisite art inside the historic buildings, within the one hundred ten-acre city state as a whole, were sufficiently detailed to occupy tourists for days. There were incredibly meticulous and polished works of art at every angle, in tall mirrors and painted ceilings. But they would not have relaxed together so easily had they known the true danger lurking in their midst.

Chapter 30

AS BIZ AND ARTHUR toured the Vatican Museums, Stewart waited outside. He restlessly watched them emerge from the shadows at the exit doors of the Museum. He was thoroughly annoyed they had taken so long to tour the buildings, and he fumed at Biz, wholly infuriated she did not seem to walk around anywhere by herself.

He knew Biz liked him. She would be sure to remember him from England because of all he had done for her. He would continue to follow her, and at the perfect moment, he planned to isolate her. In the meantime, he did not like the cameraman on her team at all and would definitely do something about him.

As he stood sulking in the sun he remembered a day long ago when he felt equally frustrated only for different reasons. He had been desperate for money because his job at the television station had not nearly covered the family's living expenses. At the initial job interview, his paunchy balding fast-talking boss named Carl gave Vince a description of work expectations in the moonlighting position if he should decide to accept it.

"I have these guys in Europe. We do everything for them, and they do nothing for us," Carl complained. "When they tell us what to do, we just have to do it. We mostly meet weekends at night. We just have to be ready whenever an opportunity presents itself. We take care of each other. That's what we do. What kind of work do you do?"

"I'm confused," said Vince simply.

"I don't want to talk about too many details," Carl said, watching Vince intently out of the corner of his eye. "You want the job? Yes or no."

Vince needed the money, so he said yes. He knew enough to know he was probably getting himself into something rough. And true enough, the jobs he was given were the types of activities he had to keep from his wife. But he needed the money and would not, could not, resign.

Stewart noticed a photographer lingering nearby taking shots of the Vatican buildings. He assumed the photographer might be a journalist or, less likely, a freelancing tourist, since he had such an impressive camera.

Stewart walked around, sometimes in the sun, varying his positions and almost shouting angry epithets out loud. He stopped and took another pill as he did when his head hurt or whenever his plans got bigger and bigger and involved more and more people. He could not wait to get his project finished.

Chapter 31

THE GOLDEN AFTERNOON sun shone majestically through immense front-facing paned glass windows. Biz sat with Arthur in a stunningly opulent restaurant surrounded by carved walnut-paneled walls and doors. The tables were furnished for lunch with impeccably clean tablecloths and silverware with cut glass goblets. High walls, extending onto an arched ceiling, had been decorated with fanciful paintings of sky-blue-and-white clouds of heavens and smiling cherubic angels, and created a spectacular effect. The lunch crowd had already moved on and the wait staff hovered, sized up customers, and anxiously tidied tables.

Biz recognized this glittering restaurant for its storied history as a renowned haunt of famous people. As a musical young girl, she had learned to play the piano and violin as well as singing, and she appreciated the Bach concertos a violinist performed in the corner of the room.

Arthur gazed into her eyes. As he glanced

below her necklaces, he lovingly remarked, "It seems a long way to Mountain Lakes when you're here, doesn't it?

"There's something you should know," he continued. "The main reason I wanted to come to Italy was to be nearer to you."

"I just don't know where this will lead," said Biz softly. "We live in different countries."

They fell into deep silence about their possible future together. Neither could be certain what might happen. On a whim she smiled and said, "You could come over to America and deliver your paintings in person, maybe meet my family."

The sun from the tall windows shined on her face. She gazed at him softly with her sapphire eyes. They peacefully drank coffee after their meal, lingering, conversing, and enjoying each other's company. Despite feeling anxious since she would soon be alone after her impending return, she stayed in extraordinary control of her emotions.

"Are you even sure you know what you do want?" asked Arthur.

"I know it's a difficult question but one I wouldn't mind exploring with you," she said.

"You have to watch what you ask for because you might get it," Arthur said carefully. Perhaps to make her think he added, "Wanting something can sometimes be more fun than actually having it."

His words alarmed Biz.

"The idea that desire can wane worries me a great deal," she said.

"Don't worry." He mischievously flashed that wicked grin he used when they first met. "You're a long way from that happening with me."

She smiled at him and reflected on his

intentions. She felt as if she could talk in depth and at length about anything with him, face him as an equal, and question any of his remarks. She had yearned for this sense of equality and healthy communication with a boyfriend all her life, and had not felt it before with anyone else.

Arthur walked her to her hotel with his arm around her shoulders. She knew he had a history of showing her he could match his words with action. This time, she invited him into her room. As he walked in, he took her into his arms.

On the inviting bed, they rapidly shed their clothes and slipped beneath the smooth embroidered cotton sheets. They were shy at first but as their passion grew, they softly moaned the words and sentiments the other had been waiting to hear. Biz felt more emboldened with excitement than she could remember having been with anyone else. The contentment she derived from his loving ministrations mended her soul, made her less lonely, and she hoped he felt the same way.

Time would tell how long they would have to stay together but, for once, they were content. They gazed into each other's eyes and felt like a couple, as if they were meant to be together. She lay on the bed most of the afternoon and hummed softly and quietly.

Biz felt deliriously satisfied and extremely guilty at taking time off work to be with him. In the late afternoon sunlight, a sparkling crystal chandelier dominated the ceiling in the air-conditioned space above a large bed with an ornate headboard. The dresser, wardrobe, and bedside tables, all were hand-painted with romantic designs like women on swings, and pets playing. She rested in his arms and felt herself slipping into a blissful state of peace and comfort with him, and she regretted nothing. By the time she finally checked the time, several hours had flown past. They quickly dressed, and on their way to dinner, passed the ancient Roman Pantheon.

As the golden sun set with rosy hues auguring fine weather on the morrow, dusty motes of light beams burned through the domed rooftop deep into the round central chamber of the ancient building, and haunted the spacious interior. Amazingly, the space remained intact, despite years of wars, tumults, and never-ending crowds of sightseers. The venerable backdrop listened in to the wide-ranging discussions of thousands of anxious visitors, just as it had for almost two millennia. The full moon revealed a bejeweled night sky and effervescent sparkling starry lights in the cloudless night.

They ventured to have a splendid romantic dinner in an intimate restaurant offering candlelight, a white tablecloth, delicious foods and wines, and violin music. They were aware of their freedom and high spirits because they were able to act as they liked, free to discuss ideas and opinions to their hearts' content.

They had agreed to meet the team briefly after dinner to coordinate activities for the next day. After all, they had new business to discuss. Details had to be reviewed concerning the impending trip to Collina Castle for the meeting of the finance ministers. Lit by flickering candles, the friendly group of five sat on light wicker chairs in the piazza outside the Pantheon. The café was furnished with simple wood chairs and iron marble tables covered with red and white checked oilcloths. Providing them with coffee and dessert, the classic café might well have been set in similar style for hundreds of years.

Biz positively glowed that evening with laughter and happiness. She reflected out loud to the group how much more she had already enjoyed this trip than her previous visits to Italy, although she had traveled through the country countless times. As crowds of Romans walked past, she remembered with pleasure the many charming evening processions or *passeggiatas* she had joined in by herself.

Landon, in a typically mellow mood, expressed awe at the sight of the well-dressed obedient children accompanying their parents for exercise. As he turned to the Piazza nearby, a solitary local at another table caught his eye. The man stared at them, with a fixed expression, as his hands played idly with his camera.

Chapter 32

AFTER LANDON TURNED back to the group puzzled, his smile turned wary, and he asked Arthur, "How do you like traveling to Italy? After all, I expect you fly a lot."

"You're right, I like to travel," said Arthur. "Italy has long been one of my favorite countries in the world. I lived here for a year with my parents as a child and used to visit the museums and art galleries. Art generally has been a way of life here in Italy for a long time. You can see examples all over the place."

"Who are your favorite painters?" Landon asked.

"My favorite artists, without doubt, are Italian: Da Vinci, Caravaggio, Raphael, Michelangelo, Tintoretto, and Canaletto. I like many others, too. Their paintings really speak to me and have an attraction I want to add to my work as a sort of philosophy." Arthur enjoyed this sort of endless conversation.

"Everything men and women want," Arthur

continued, "has hardly changed at all through many centuries of human existence, no matter how enlightened and progressive we think we are. In relationships, we all have to weed through the unconscious expectations and assumptions we make of each other, however inconsistent. These are important issues in any relationship: how much emotional trust we have for each other; our capacity for intimacy, since we're all different; and how much recognition we need to have. In our relationships, we're at our best and our worst. In the final analysis, I think we're all more alike than we're different."

Biz smiled, along with all of them, relieved he so closely echoed her own sentiments. And nothing approached having friends, associates in this case, approving of one's boyfriend to heighten romantic interest. They attributed his philosophical exposition to the hot Italian climate, the wine, and the sultry evening air, and listened with friendly curiosity to the continuing discussions.

That night, Arthur walked Biz back to the hotel. They held hands, arms encircling each other's waist, and walked through the mist talking endlessly.

"I'd like to hear more about your philosophy, if you will, about love," she said quietly, as she looked up at him.

"It's easy once you realize everyone wants to love others and be loved. My philosophy when I'm traveling," he continued, "is incredibly simple. It's this: you only need to love others. Here's a famous anonymous quotation: 'What most people need to learn in life is how to love people and use things, instead of using people and loving things.'"

Biz pursued his thought by mentioning a parallel observation in the form of a question. "Have you ever loved someone more than another person loved you?"

"Many, many people I've liked have not mirrored back their feelings and felt exactly the same way," he agreed. "It's sad but I suppose it happens to everyone to some extent."

"Do you believe in true love?"

He turned to Biz and paused before he nodded and replied, slowly and carefully. "I do believe it happens," he said. "Luckily, it happens in reverse as well. Sometimes you might not be aware of it when others love you."

Just before entering the hotel, she invited Arthur to sleep in her room again, and he accepted with pleasure. Having some private hours alone could only help push along their relationship. They snuggled together in the sheets to muffled sounds of traffic outside. They were wholly intent on giving each other pleasure. They knew they did not have much time together, but what they had was extremely intense. They stayed afterward lying next to each other, knees knotted together, arms and legs wound around, for as long as they could.

He had placed a wedge into her soul; her career merged with his life. She opened her mind and heart to him despite any possible consequences to her own personal security.

The next morning in Rome, Biz awoke deeply happy and smiled sleepily. Arthur had stayed with her in her room although he had his own room downstairs. She turned around, tickled his arm, and enjoyed being in bed with him a while longer. She craved more of his time and attention. They could not get enough of each other, and made the most of their time together before they had to meet the others and start the day. Only then did he go to his own room where he had left his bag.

She worried she might be late for work, as she brushed her teeth, and not have enough time to prepare for her working day as she usually did. She would need several cups of coffee to face the world. For work, she had to plan ahead and review her notes.

As she checked the weather outside, she knew a walk around would do her a world of good, but decided it would have to wait. Not feeling sufficiently confident to venture far by herself, she made a wish. She would ask Arthur if he might be interested in a ride with her on a horse-drawn carriage around the old city sometime, though not that morning. She wanted to make more time in her schedule for him. To her surprise, she had fallen in love. Yet she had certain objections to handle before she could commit more fully to any relationship.

Biz ventured alone into the coffee shop downstairs in the hotel, and waited to have coffee with Arthur. The strong morning sun filtered in through a bay window past thick damask curtains as she sat upon a red velvet bench. Miraculously, she could read her recent emails on her cell phone. She was relieved there were not any urgent messages to feel guilty about missing.

She happened to walk to the windows where she found a table, ordered strong cappuccinos for both of them, and skimmed through her notes. She typically enjoyed contemplating the soothing rhythm of the private lives of families wherever she happened to be. Italian mothers walked past her window with their children. Most of the children ran along by themselves to school. But a few mothers with time and energy to spare also walked together talking. As if in slow motion, the overall impression appeared achingly touching, even as she recognized the disparate path of her own life journey so far.

She stretched into a sinuous yawn as she calmly sat enjoying the scene. That vision, of the ordinary daily lives she had just seen, remained etched in her memory within a soft private cloud. Reminiscing in her secret dream of safe peaceful domesticity, she hazily gazed into Arthur's eyes when he reappeared. He sat opposite, and nodded gratefully to her for ordering his coffee. He added several teaspoons of sugar, picked up the cup of brew, and calmly sipped the strong roasted liquid.

Her thoughts concentrated into a focused snap as breaking news flashed on the nearby television screen in Italian. She turned to see a special report about a major jewelry heist. Although she could not understand every word, she watched the pictures and listened with intense interest. Photographs, enlarged in high definition, showed treasured silver with intricate designs from unnamed ecclesiastical sources, and holy rings made of fine chalcedony jewels. Shining rubies and sparkling sapphires flashed on the screen. Evidently a ring of thieves had broken into a Banco Lazio branch, the bank exactly across the street from them near the Vatican, and taken from their vaults pieces of unique artistic silver pieces and pricey religious gems.

"This Banco Lazio happens to be the exact

location of the robbery." Biz was stunned. "And it's the bank in which we'll interview the bank president, Giuseppe Angelini, a little later in the day. I could use some cash if they'll let us. Would you mind helping me get in to see it immediately?"

"Yes, of course. We could investigate if you like. Do you have enough time?"

"Just barely," she said. "We could go now. I'll need to work with the others on the interview until late afternoon. Thanks for being such a good friend."

He had followed her research with focused interest, and would enjoy this mission to follow a possible story lead with her, and offer his professional advice.

They wandered like tourists to the bank where uniformed police officers heavily guarded the entrance. The bank appeared to be conducting business as usual with an extra layer of security.

"I need to use the machine to withdraw some money *per favore*," Biz enquired politely to the policemen. "I need to go inside."

With a grudging nod of confirmation, an officer politely tipped his hat and opened the door to allow them to enter.

"Isn't it just beautiful?" she asked Arthur.

The immense hall with ornate ironwork dazzled them. High ceilings had been lavishly painted. Angels in clouds and decorations of cherubs in relief were formed from plaster. It was difficult to imagine how a break-in had succeeded through the thick iron doors of the vault set into a side wall.

After Biz completed her transaction, they returned to the hotel. They walked with their arms interlaced.

"Thank you so much for doing this with me," she said as she gave him a hug.

"Happy to oblige," said Arthur with a grin.

When they had almost entered the hotel, they had to bid farewell again.

She remembered pages she had to read to make questions before the interview. She planned to try to follow up the theft, and had to meet the others for the televised interview and focus urgently on the present.

"I'm sorry but now I simply must turn my thoughts to this interview. The team should be waiting here in the lobby."

To her relief, Arthur did not appear to mind in the least. "Don't worry, I have some art friends to speak to," he said. "Call me when you're ready later. Otherwise, let's meet around five in the lobby."

Biz kissed him before they parted, and walked with him until she met her coworkers in the lobby. She needed to research the bank and question executives but found her mind wandering. Her heart followed Arthur as he left to visit art galleries.

Biz had to focus on her upcoming interview with the bank president. Leaning on her connections, she reached his office the same morning to confirm the appointment. Before she held the interview, she handled a call from the head office back in the States to congratulate her on the stories. The quality of her work had actually improved while she was abroad working with Arthur. She found this news deliciously pleasing.

Chapter 33

THE TEAM FROM WYN-TV entered the front offices of Banco Lazio and passed beyond the ironwork gate Biz had noticed earlier. The president's secretary led them past elaborate wrought-iron screens, tall green malachite pillars with gold Corinthian capitals, across shiny marble floors. Through impressively carved thick metal partition doors, they walked behind the scenes into the inner sanctum. Along dark wooded hallways, heavily paneled-wood walls were lit with elaborate sconces. An ancient door opened to reveal the office of the president and once inside they were led across a vast expanse to a giant lavishly carved mahogany desk, gleaming in glowing golden lamplight, empty of paperwork save a few Italian desk accessories. One at a time, they shook hands with Giuseppe Angelini.

As Biz shook his hand, she noticed his wavy black hair. Appropriately, he wore a pin-striped business suit, blue silk shirt and tie, and shiny leather dress shoes.

The team members were efficient at their tasks and did not waste a moment. Landon set up bright lights, and took videos of the ceilings and floors of the ornately decorated office. Gina fussed while placing a microphone on him, and adjusted it considerately for his comfort.

Jessie turned to Biz, camera in hand, focused, and whispered, "Your turn. Take it from here. Five-four-three-two-one."

Biz raised her chin in a characteristic gesture as she stood to face the camera and began her report.

"Here in Rome with Giuseppe Angelini, President of Banco Lazio. I'm hoping to learn details about the Italian economy. Thank you for speaking with us, Signor Angelini."

At the televised introductory greeting, he smiled his perfect dazzling teeth into the camera. His name and the bank logo appeared printed on the screen below his picture. To conduct the interview, Biz sat her guest on his two green leather chairs, perfectly color-matching the green malachite architectural details.

Jessie and Gina stood behind the camera and focused on her report. They were all aware that much of the bank's business connected them with the hospitality industry's hotels, restaurants and food stores. One wall in his office showed an impressive array of signed photographs of Signor Angelini. In them, he was shaking hands with business owners and clerics posing in lines, probably at awards dinners.

Biz turned to him to ask questions for her interview. "What do you see ahead for businesses in Italy? How are your numbers looking?"

"The numbers are fine for the late summer season. We had a record number of foreign visitors, and businesses report they made money despite the higher cost of energy and rising rents."

"Americans are still coping with the results of the downturn in the economy even now as the stock market is improving. Travel is down; home buying is at a new low. Do you foresee a better winter ahead or do you think Europeans generally, and Italians especially, are cutting travel?"

"We see an Italian consumer interested in the food business, in fashion, in businesses and jobs, in tourism, wines and olive oils. We see a robust bounce in the economy in the next few quarters at a minimum. Northern European customers flood our cities, again and again, every summer."

"Are banks liquid enough to lend money, so consumers can borrow to buy houses?"

"The Italian economy doesn't rely on citizens receiving tax credits for mortgages, taking money borrowed in loans from their houses, and investing it in the stock market, as America does. The housing market is stable, and is likely to stay that way for the foreseeable future."

"Signor Angelini, your bank suffered a major art theft last night. Can you tell me any news concerning how exactly the thieves managed to enter the bank?"

"No, I'm sorry," he said politely.

"Did they leave anything behind?"

"I cannot comment because there is an ongoing official investigation. Perhaps you should question the police. The paintings taken have been held by the bank for many years and were constantly monitored as their value increased substantially. The bank is taking the security lapse very seriously. We are upgrading the system today since it happened overnight."

"Thank you very much for having us, Signor Angelini, for answering our questions, and for your time. We wish you all the best with your challenges."

They smiled, and briefly shook hands.

Landon swiveled the camera, and focused his lens solely on Biz.

"The latest news from Signor Giuseppe Angelini, President of Banco Lazio, one of Italy's largest banks: reporting good news on the Italian economy. Sending it back, this is Biz Andrews for WYN-TV."

The screen returned to the previously scheduled two-hour program in New York. Biz thanked Signor Angelini once again after the camera had been turned off and the televised interview ended. She had not injected her own opinions on the Italian economy during the interview, and had expected him to be relentlessly upbeat and optimistic, which he was.

She lifted a sign on his otherwise cleared desk, and beheld the familiar crest of the Diamondbacks.

"Was this sign left after the theft?" she asked, surprised to see a photocopy.

"I will confirm, off the record, as you say in America, it was probably carried out by the Diamondbacks." Rather abruptly, he accompanied them to the heavily carved door of his office. "Thank you. I'm sure you understand. I have pressing business now."

Biz had hoped for more information for her viewers. She had been lucky to obtain the interview, but did not show surprise when he refused to comment publicly regarding the theft. At some point, opening banks to the public with such news could interfere with the bank's central mission to protect their reputations. With tight security being at the heart of that historic mission, thefts of any kind could not have been good for business.

Chapter 34

STEWART FOCUSED his pathetically warped attention laser-like directly on Biz. If she did not have one man with her, she had another. How could he get her alone, he groaned to himself. He had endured weeks and weeks now of thwarted attempts.

She had such a prosperous life; she stayed in expensive hotels, ate in the best restaurants, and did it often enough to make anyone jealous, he sniffed. She most definitely did not deserve so much when he had nothing.

He remembered back to the time he had started his part-time job with the Diamondbacks, when he and Darla began to think about buying a place in a better suburb where rich people lived. They had dreamed of buying a three-story house on an acre, with pillars at the front, and its own garage. They wanted a better lifestyle, and they accepted a mortgage from a company with an incredible interest rate.

He was soon able to move his family into a

larger house, though not as fancy as they had hoped. Not enormous, it had a better address than his last one. His parents would not have liked him being farther away from them, or in the business at all. In a short time, he owed the syndicate and bought almost everything new on credit.

Making money to support a more expensive lifestyle for Darla and his family drove him further into the black hole of debt in which he had already fallen. His secretiveness about his activities bothered his sweet wife. After a while, his crazy hours and mysterious jobs became too much for her. She started to notice his side business had to do with pornography, and that Vince stayed awake late spending weeknights at his computer. She noticed he would not talk about his job, and she did not approve. He left home unexpectedly at all hours and racked up extra miles on his car.

The job became the final straw that ultimately unraveled their home life and drove a hard wedge into their marriage. It was only a matter of time before his wife forced him to move out of the family home, and his resentment of his situation had remained raw ever since.

If he could not get to Biz just yet, he would at least take something away from her. Something that would hurt her. Something else she valued. He already had the planner and the watch.

He definitely did not like the man who set up the camera and followed her around. Something had to change, he said to himself. He would make sure that soon Biz should have more material for reports than the entire staff of WYN-TV could handle.

In the lobby of the luxurious palazzo hotel, Biz and Landon were comfortably set at separate marble tables. They pored over their laptops, workdays officially ended, absorbed in their reading and personal email. Biz researched a post about a variety of financial angles concerning women's issues to write about on her online site. She hoped writing about her own financial challenges helped her viewers. She was also waiting for Arthur, and had been assured he would arrive there soon.

Landon had been her trusted ally for years and a constant presence at WYN-TV. Unerringly polite, he took photos and videos of her reports and usefully obtained introductions to many of the financial mavens she wanted to interview. His travel and technical expertise finessed some of the European interviews. Her relationship with him remained businesslike at all times and she did not push her luck with his generous nature. They both hoped to move up in the company.

Content to draw a decent salary, Landon derived a sense of pride as a steady husband and a fine father. His family defined the parameters of his conscience. Coretta and the children were the heart and soul of his life, and consumed much of his energy. He did not always travel with the crew but this time he had done so because of the importance of the trip. A half hour later, they were still in the lobby, busy on their computers. Arthur had not appeared.

Landon turned to Biz with concern in his voice. "There's a guy following us wherever we go. I didn't want to think about it but he's appeared in other places. I'm certain now although I'd been wondering. I'm almost sure I saw him in England and France. Now, he just watches us, and takes photos. He must have our itinerary. It couldn't be a coincidence. He isn't following us everywhere, and only when you're around. I've seen him stare at you. Then he stands around and talks on his phone. He often takes a quick photo our way, hides behind someone, and disappears. He just vanishes until he reappears somewhere else on our route."

Biz froze at his words. She had already advised Landon about her follower in the blue hat as well as her string of losses, her daily planner, and her watch, and was grateful for his presence.

She was also glad Arthur had assured her he was on his way to meet her. She would appreciate his protective support.

"Thanks for telling me, although I'm not sure what to do, being in Italy. I think I would call the police if we were in America. Which one is he?"

"Do you see the dude with a professional camera next to the lady in the red dress?"

Landon pointed out a sun-tanned local wearing a black outfit, t-shirt, and jeans. He resembled any number of Italian men.

"What do you think we should do?" she asked. Her backbone shivered with fright.

"Not sure, either. I just wanted to tell you. I think I'll call the office. He doesn't seem dangerous, just suspicious. I hope it's nothing and I'm making it up."

Biz shuddered, shaken to her core. "I hadn't noticed him before but I've had a quick peek at him now. I'm glad we're going to be away from here on our excursion tomorrow. I'll keep my eye out for him."

Biz happened to glance around her shoulder again to check whether their unknown follower had lingered. A shadow crossed her line of vision. She happened to raise her head slowly, and gasped at the sight of Lord Dawson's driver.

Stewart stood in front of her, nervously shaking, and stared at her transfixed. He looked at Landon briefly, and then turned his attention back to her.

"This is an unexpected and pleasant surprise. How are you?" she asked, as she logged off her computer. She turned her attention to Stewart and felt instantly safer at the familiar sight. The man in the distance receded from her vision and fled her mind temporarily.

"Fine. You? I wouldn't want to disturb you," he said politely.

Stewart had lost a great deal of weight since she had last seen him, and appeared haggard and anxious.

"Coffee?" she asked him. "Here, please sit down. So…why are you in Italy?" she asked as he sat in a chair next to her.

"Thanks. I'm in a hurry and don't have much time. I'm driving Lord Dawson around. The traffic's demanding and I needed a break. So when I saw you, I wanted to say hello. I thought you were alone," he said casually. He sat in a chair at her table where he could get a perfect view of both Biz and Landon. "His name slips my mind, I'm sorry."

"Landon. He's our cameraman. He works with me." She wondered if they were staying in the same hotel.

He stared hungrily at her handbag. "Nice bag. It must be genuine alligator unless it's crocodile."

She looked at him puzzled. "Crocodile actually," she said.

She liked him and wondered if working for Lord Dawson was stressful for him. He seemed so jittery, as if he could do with a square meal. She wondered sympathetically if he was hungry and suddenly felt thirsty herself.

"Just a moment, please. I'm going to get us some coffee and desserts. Keep an eye on my bag for me?" She trusted Stewart.

She took her wallet and other contents from her bag, placed them on the table, and walked over to the front desk. Her heels clattered on the marble floor as she walked away, attracting attention, as usual.

Chapter 35

BY THE TIME Biz returned with a tray, Stewart had disappeared. She had pastries, water, and three tiny sugary espressos in white china, and looked around puzzled.

"Did you see Stewart leave?" she asked Landon, seated nearby.

The lobby of the modern hotel had turned quiet, and she counted church bells tolling the hour five times. She expected Arthur any minute.

"He probably just went to visit the rest room," he replied.

When Stewart did not return, she assumed he had been called away, with no time to find her and tell her. Being a driver was probably like that. He had to run on a moment's notice whenever the boss needed him.

"Odd the way he appeared in front of me, almost like a ghost. I barely recognized his face, and he didn't warn me he had to go so fast," Biz said. "He didn't look well."

Landon simply shrugged in response and said,

"I didn't really notice. Though to be honest, I was a bit glad he left. I wonder if he's taking drugs. Did you notice he was shaking as he spoke to you?"

Biz sighed. She really didn't know Stewart very well, and would have to chalk this up to an unsolved mystery. She opened her handbag to place her wallet and papers inside.

"Where's my passport?" she asked him. "You didn't take it, did you?"

"Of course not. I've been zoned out online. Maybe the hotel staff has it. There've been guests passing your table. Any one of them could have taken it. Happens a lot in Europe." He looked at her with sympathy, slightly embarrassed he had not noticed. And he certainly did not want to believe it had been stolen.

She looked dizzily at him. Her positive upbeat mood vanished and she began to panic. She quickly walked to the front desk again. She told them someone must have stolen her passport. She hoped she had made a mistake. Perhaps the office of the hotel had safely hidden it. What other bad luck could befall her, she wondered.

The front desk advised her to wait and summoned the police. She had, luckily, left a paper copy of it in her suitcase, felt somewhat relieved to remember that she had done so, and retrieved it from her room. She met the police in the lobby when they arrived at the hotel to question her, and showed them her copy. While worried about the possibility of identity theft, she could do nothing to prevent it at that stage. She still had her wallet and credit cards, so her cash flow was fine. The theft could have been far worse.

The American Embassy later told her a new

passport would soon be ready for pick up. The whole episode did not become the disaster it might have been. She hoped a new copy would be done before her return trip to America in a couple of days.

She felt shocked and hoped Stewart's visit had nothing to do with her missing passport. He had seemed such a nice man. She did not want to believe he could have taken her passport, although he had not seemed like himself. She had not remembered to ask where he and Lord Dawson were staying, and so the question of whether Stewart remembered seeing it was irrelevant.

More likely, the photographer that Landon had mentioned earlier had taken it. The one she had seen with her own eyes. So much for her famously clear vision, she thought wryly. She would watch out for the man they had seen, and stay more careful in general.

Arthur had appeared by then, and he reassured her that after this, he would walk around everywhere with her. She would not have to go out by herself at all.

Biz and Arthur had a late dinner alone together that evening, after he met her at the hotel. Despite still feeling flushed with fear, she found the restaurant romantic, and was grateful for his presence.

"Thank you for this meal," she said solicitously. "I'm still shaken from the shock of having my passport stolen. It's the latest in a string of bad luck, and it's probably best to put it out of my mind."

"I hope it'll be the last one," he said kindly. "You'll have your new one very soon, don't worry.

It's happened to me, too. Unfortunately, passports are stolen and sold all the time. There's nothing new about it. Bad things happen to good people."

In the candlelight, she considered the kind words of the attractive man across the table from her. In the splendid room with detailed paintings of cherubs in clouds on the ceiling, she finally relaxed as she sipped a mellow taste of fine shiraz.

Chapter 36

ARTHUR PLANNED TO accompany the team up the mountains to Collina Castle and watch the meeting of the bankers the next day. They were driven, along with their equipment, in a large hired van along the narrow cobblestone streets. After passing through Rome up to the ancient town of Collina, the van ascended even higher. They zigzagged left, right, left, right, slowly upward. The narrow road proved extremely hazardous. Everyone hoped they would not meet another vehicle coming down in the opposite direction, although they did a few times. The driver, as a natural consequence, repeatedly denied their requests to stop, to allow them to take photos of the panoramic views.

As the van gained altitude passing craggy rocks and lush verdant valleys, an incredible vista extended all the way to the sparkling blue Mediterranean Sea. The breathtaking scene in azure, her favorite color, flickered with shimmering silvery reflections below the blazing sun. Biz quickly snapped an unforgettable image through the artistically smeary window in her cell phone and did not expect the photo to begin to capture the magnificence of the view.

Arriving at the summit a few minutes early for the meeting, she sat with Arthur in the gentle sunshine at an outdoor café in the piazza of the castle. They had ordered steaming cups of latte in the comfortably breezy weather. Luckily, she could drink coffee all day and the caffeine rarely bothered her sleep.

Arthur turned and asked to borrow a British newspaper from a man sitting at the next table if he had finished reading it, since English-language newspapers were scarce. The man wearing a business suit looked at them kindly. On his lawn-green tie, Biz's almost perfect vision picked up the amusing pattern of flying pink baby elephants. Arthur casually placed his arm on her knee for a few moments, and they chuckled with amusement. She wanted to tell her friends they shared the same sense of humor.

The banker noticed their mirth, although not its' source. To her surprise, he smiled at her and caught her attention with a wave. "I recognize you from New York. I'm Charles Peterson. You've interviewed me on air once. Do you remember?"

She felt pleased he had recognized her, and looked at him quizzically. She was not surprised to hear he was American, his outfit should have given it away. She chose to respond to him with her most polite professional smile.

"It was at the golf tournament in South Carolina," he added, to jog her memory. "I went there to play golf after the G20 meeting."

He seemed sunny and good-natured. She was embarrassed as she recognized him. "I'm sorry, yes; I do remember the interview now. Thank you for reminding me. You and your wife went to Columbia, didn't you? How is Marylou?"

"She's fine, at home with our boys. Ross is five and Lance is three already. When I'm away from them, my life slows down. I certainly miss them when I travel."

"I'm sure you do. Time flies...Your wife was heading for a career in business, if my memory is correct," Biz said.

"Good memory. She started a company that makes fruit smoothies and has franchises around the Northeast," he said. "How are you doing? Enjoying Europe?"

"I'm still in shock because I lost my passport yesterday. I'm waiting for a replacement," she said.

"It shouldn't take long. When these annoyances happen they have a tendency to slow us down and wonder why they happened, whether maybe someone needed a tip or something. It's probably not anything personal. You were probably just in the wrong place at the wrong time," he said.

"Thank you. That's nice to hear. It's upsetting me. We don't know who stole it."

"A setback you didn't need."

"I'll try not to let it bother me. Thanks for your sympathy."

"Passport thefts, unfortunately, happen all over the world," he said. "Anyway, you're doing great. We enjoy watching whenever we see you on television."

"Thank you again very much. By the way, I want to find out more about an Italian banker I interviewed yesterday, Giuseppe Angelini. Have you met him? I saw a sign of the Diamondbacks in his office after a jewelry theft at his bank and wondered why it was there."

"Oh yes. There's a rumor he is an enemy of the Diamondbacks, which would make him a good guy."

"Thanks very much, I'm glad to hear you've met him. This is Arthur Deephart, a British expert on the world of art. He's traveling with us while we report on the art heists."

The men exchanged greetings.

"I'd like to know more of what Mr. Angelini knows about the Diamondbacks," said Biz. "He seems like a quiet private person. Would you mind calling me if you find out anything?"

"Certainly. I'll see what I can do." He obviously felt flattered to be asked a favor by a famous television reporter.

"Have you heard anything about the Diamondbacks around here?" asked Biz, while Arthur listened in.

"Not much. I've heard the Diamondbacks are involved in major jewelry and art heists," said Charles. "They were behind a big one in Monaco last year and another in Spain. Global law enforcement authorities have been searching for them. In every case, they left their distinctive sign behind inside the bank. They always work overnight and they dismantle security systems."

"We need more solid information. We don't know where they live, unfortunately, or even who they are," said Biz.

"Based on my talks with Giuseppe, this is what I know. They're situated in many countries and always help one another. Typically, they're models of civilized behavior and solid respected members of their communities. They could work anywhere, as owners of restaurants, asphalt pavers, scrap metal workers.

"It must be very complicated to steal and transport large paintings." Biz said. "The Diamondbacks must have to know details about complex wiring and unpredictable security systems."

Charles leaned in, and nodded his head. "Absolutely. Their day jobs are just fronts. That's the sense I have but I don't know very much about them."

"Thank you very much," Biz leaned over to the friendly banker, grateful. "Here's my card. Call me and stay in touch."

His information had helped shed some light on the secretive Diamondbacks. But this was not his job. Biz did not expect to hear from him in the near future. She needed answers now. Real-time demands at the television station would not readily permit long-term exploratory research. The competitive needs of the station, to have facts, and make money from increased viewer volume, pushed journalists like her ahead. If she did not find the facts, someone else might find them before her.

Biz and Arthur wanted to spend all their time together, and again found themselves in that predicament of Biz having to move on, unsure when they could meet again. The tension distracted them.

After the group returned to the hotel in Rome, they had a late dinner together in an intimate restaurant, one of Arthur's favorites. Violin music played familiar Italian laments. Rome abounded with such establishments, romantically lit with candles, pretty flowers, and white china on immaculate, pressed tablecloths, and they made the most of their time together.

They strolled slowly to the hotel after their meal, with their arms folded around each other in the moist evening air. Oblivious to the glances of passing strangers, Biz listened intensely to Arthur's breathing, savoring every last moment.

She asked him her last secret request with light trepidation, "Could we please have a ride on the horse carriage sometime before we leave?" Urgency weakened her voice. For some reason, she expected him to turn her down.

"Yes, of course, we can," he said, and they stopped and kissed each other.

Arthur stayed with her during the final leg of her European trip. They tried to make up ahead of time in bed for the days they would not be together. She went to sleep and awoke with him that last morning. They enjoyed their unique and private moments together.

They had been able to make it to the American Consulate to have a new passport issued. There was no doubt now she would be leaving for America.

Expecting to hurry to visit sights before they had to leave, they took the promised carriage ride that Biz had been hoping for. Sitting at a great height, they liked how much of Rome they could see in slow motion. It was another highlight of their eventful visit to the ancient city.

They also visited ecclesiastical sites and art galleries to refresh themselves on Italian art. Grand churches showed art of religious visions, of deep and abiding faith. The sun flowed like golden syrup through prisms in stained glass windows. Beautiful rainbows of bright colors created shadows on the opposite walls. Paintings at Santa Maria Maggiore almost overwhelmed them. The organ played haunting melodies and hymns quietly. A few tourists wandered about, and a few of the faithful at the front lit votive candles. There were too many churches and historic sites to see. They had to cut many from her list they would have liked to visit.

Biz could imagine traveling to an almost infinite number of places with Arthur. She could imagine a future with him bursting with complex possibilities, if only they could figure out a way to be together.

As she finally packed her bags to go to America, she gazed sadly at Arthur in her luxurious hotel room replete with crystal chandeliers, murals painted with elaborate flower designs, and ceilings plastered with whimsical cherubs. She loved Italy and would be sorry to leave. She would surely miss this hotel where they had shared passion and made love. But she would miss him a lot more.

She turned to him when he wanted to keep his hands on her and took his hands tenderly. They hungrily kissed as he pulled her onto the bed one last time. They would have to trust they would be together again soon.

She grew heartbroken with emotion and had to dab away all her stray tears when the time came to hurry to the lobby of the hotel where Jessie and Gina awaited her.

Chapter 37

LANDON WAS MISSING under mysterious circumstances.

Jessie and Gina were agitated. They had met him for breakfast the day before, then headed out to shop all day without him. Later in the evening before dinner they had knocked on his hotel door after they had been shopping. He had not bothered to answer his door or his cell phone, a move that was highly uncharacteristic of him. Since they were supposed to return to America the next day they were not unduly alarmed. They assumed he had taken a last dash around the city, probably for the same reasons they had.

But Landon still had not made an appearance in the lobby of the hotel the next morning. Biz conversed with Jessie and Gina about his absence. They wondered why he was not packed and ready to travel with them to the airport from the hotel. The ladies had to board the plane to America without him, and remained totally mystified by his absence.

It took a few days until WYN-TV and his

family in America officially decided he had not returned. His disappearance was considered mysterious by all who cared about him. His wife, Coretta, began proceedings to order a formal investigation to find out where he had disappeared and what could have happened to him.

Chapter 38

ALONE IN HER OFFICE, Biz answered her phone.

"Too busy to talk?" Arthur asked politely.

"It's a good time, Arthur, thank you," she said.

"Dining *al desko*? It's close to supper time over here."

Biz heard herself sigh. Either from the comfort of his voice or the heaviness of her heart, she didn't know. Since she desired more privacy, she stood up and quietly shut her office door.

"How are you?" he asked.

"We got the news today. Some hotel cleaner found Landon in his room too late. He was bound with a cloth belt and duct tape and gagged with a bandana. The police inspected his body and the hotel room and could not find any sign of fingerprints whatsoever in his room."

"I'm so sorry. How did it happen?"

"How did he die? He was injected with a lethal dose of potassium chloride."

WYN-TV was flying its office flag at half-mast. Biz was keeping the pain of losing her friend quiet but sometimes she burst into tears at unexpected moments.

"That's not the end of it either. I heard today investigators found the DB insignia of the Diamondbacks on a man's bracelet. I saw a picture of the bracelet, which rang a bell, but I can't remember where I've seen it before. "

"Do you think Landon was one of them?"

"He couldn't be. He was a family man. Worked around the clock sometimes. Besides he didn't wear a bracelet."

"Yes, but the Diamondbacks, as a rule, present themselves as respectable hard-working citizens."

"You met Landon. You saw he is—was—a good person."

"I apologize. You're absolutely right but the alternative..."

"The alternative being that he was an innocent man bound and killed by a powerful secret organization?"

"An innocent man who was close to you, a high-profile news reporter investigating the Diamondbacks' connection to the art thefts and jewelry heists."

"You think they were sending me a signal?"

"Maybe Landon wasn't a Diamondback, and now that I think about it I don't believe he was, but at some point a Diamondback was in his room before, during, or after his death. They were either after something he had or they were trying to send you or WYN-TV a message."

"I really hope the Italian police can figure this out. We're commissioning an official investigation to help his wife Coretta."

"I wish I were there now. You need to be cheered up. I expect to visit next month."

Biz smiled when she heard his words and exhaled with relief.

"I was hoping you could come," she said. "I wanted my family to meet you." She paused. Further changing the mood of the conversation, she added with humor, "I'm still waiting for your paintings. What about them?"

"I'm bringing them with me and will be happy to make a personal delivery," he said. "Two weekends after your Thanksgiving."

"That's very close to Christmas," Biz noticed as she briefly referred to a calendar. "Would you like to stay and meet my family? I take time off between Christmas and New Year every year, if I possibly can. We can all have Christmas together. My family would welcome you here."

"Thank you. That's such a kind invitation. I used to spend my Christmases with my grandmother after my parents died. But she passed away last year and the thought of having my birthday, the day before Christmas, and Christmas alone, is my idea of a nightmare. I thought it would be better to travel and even better if I could visit you."

"I'm very sorry to hear about your grandmother. How does flying in to JFK Airport and meeting by the waterfall at Trump Tower in Manhattan sound? Actually, when I think about it, I have a better idea. Instead of staying in New York, why don't you just fly to Newark Airport, deliver the paintings, and stay at my townhouse in Mountain Lakes with me," she said. "We'll go to New York, see the sights, and celebrate your birthday and the holidays together for the first time."

After they ended the call, Biz felt her spirits lift as much as they could have in her grief. She would certainly welcome a visit from Arthur. Her heart beat faster at the thought of it. In fact, she could hardly wait to meet him again, this time on home turf.

Chapter 39

ARTHUR ARRIVED on a mid-December Friday evening in a limousine directly from Newark Airport, heavily laden with two large parcels. He kissed her passionately at her front door and they made love there and then, before she had a chance to see the paintings.

That night the lightning and thunderous roar of a passing storm masked their hungry sounds of passion in the bedroom. Arthur could not keep his hands off her, and Biz did not want him to. They fell into a love haze of their own making, as if the rest of the world did not exist. They truly did not need anyone else. Their lovemaking continued unabated, and they took up where they had left off, intensely craving more of the other's time and attention. The strong emotions they felt for each other had not waned after their travels in Europe.

The next morning at nine, they were driven into New York City by limousine to see art stores and galleries by appointment. Biz dressed down in designer jeans, a multi-colored wide scarf over a high-necked cardigan, and genuine crocodile cowboy boots. Arthur wore jeans, a blue shirt, and a tweed jacket.

Since Biz knew Arthur wanted to take in museums or even private galleries, she had made appointments with gallery owners in the city. The owners jumped at the chance to meet him and discuss the latest news rocking the art world. The pair could easily have filled countless weeks just exploring Manhattan and agreed to return, which they did for the next few days.

Before Biz introduced him to her family she felt it important to have time alone with him. They had an especially enjoyable lunch one day, Viennese style, in the Neue Galerie on Fifth Avenue and admired the tall mirrors, impressive windows, and fancy woodwork as they lingered in the flowing golden sunlight. They talked about his work and where he might one day show his paintings. To her relief, he reassured her that he enjoyed hearing her American accent in the midst of so many others.

"I'm glad you came. I wanted to have more time with you. The last couple of weeks have been hard on all of us but especially Landon's family. Coretta is a mess understandably. And we still don't have the answers we need."

"Has there been any clearer evidence of the Diamondback connection?"

"No, though some people are worried about rumors. About a decade ago our station had to fire a cameraman involved in criminal activities. He was supposed to go to prison but he escaped probably onto a boat. It was that same case my father prosecuted. The one we talked about."

"They're beginning to wonder if Landon was a

Diamondback connected to the cameraman and killed by one of them?"

"Just people who didn't know Landon well. Makes me furious."

"Sometimes you may think you know a person thoroughly, only to find the other person has hidden a lot away."

He remembered his friend Sarah in England who had seemed so open and kind at first, and then had proven in time to be a controlling person.

Biz sighed. She was emotionally exhausted from weeks of asking herself these same questions. She changed the topic. "If you didn't paint, what do you think you would do?"

"Let me see, if I didn't paint…" This time it was his voice trailing off. "I'm already consulting about art theft but the market is rather small for that. Maybe I'd open an art gallery and help other artists sell their works. To be a better artist, a name people say when they discuss the best artists in the world, I'd have to devote all my time to it. I'd rather be an artist than almost anything else because I wouldn't have the interest. Every day I work on some project. That's not saying much, being a solitary artist, but sometimes I work sixteen hours a day. No matter what, I feel better after I've painted a few hours every day."

Arthur spoke faster and faster, passionately. "That's the beauty of my career. It's portable, it's flexible, and I could travel with you. My remaining properties are now for sale. I don't need them. I don't have to be in any particular location to paint as long as I have my tools."

"I like that," said Biz. She suddenly felt very aroused and she could scarcely contain her excitement. Arthur made her feel frisky and the city itself had a way of doing that to her, with all the crowds around her, but she would have to wait.

As they returned to her house together in the limousine, they enthusiastically made plans for the remainder of his trip. He would finally meet her family at Warm Springs Farm. But first, they would have the whole night to themselves. He made her uneasy feelings, her fears of being stalked, dissolve.

Chapter 40

THE DAY BEFORE Christmas, Biz and Arthur together visited the town of Lambertville mainly to shop and visit the galleries. They celebrated his birthday all day long. They had been spending a few days driving around New Jersey. Biz introduced him to her parents and showed off a few of her favorite haunts.

There were seasonal decorations and displays all around the town. Wide red-and-green ribbons and huge shiny glass balls hung from evergreen trees. Green laurel swags adorned doors, stair rails, and banisters. Carols played constantly in new variations. The decorative effects certainly fit Arthur's preconceptions of an "old-fashioned" American Christmas.

The charming storybook town complete with gourmet organic restaurants, Victorian frame houses with sturdy stone foundations, and a few significantly historic stone houses and churches, piqued his interest. They visited art galleries in and around Lambertville and discovered about ten of them in total.

Biz admired Arthur's shrewd business instincts as he inspected and researched paintings. He searched by name of artist, quality, age, price, history, previous owners, and their provenance. The galleries tended to specialize in different periods but they found three of them in his niche to visit. The British owner of the Four Color Art Gallery, a hip gallery where paintings generally used far more than four colors, recognized Arthur immediately and energetically welcomed him on this impromptu visit. They agreed to email each other about a possible show of his art in the future.

To Arthur's evident amusement and gratitude, her parents celebrated his birthday with an American birthday cake and candles. They traditionally waited until Christmas Day to open their presents. And he appreciated their attention and generosity.

Secretly, Biz almost dreaded facing her family at Christmas another year still unmarried, and was grateful for Arthur's presence. She had not liked being alone in past years when Dean had insisted on going alone to celebrate Christmas with his family. She had always gone to hers by herself. She found Christmas the one time of year when she did not wish to travel far if she could possibly avoid it. She craved the warmth of home and hearth in the holidays, and loved and respected her family. She appreciated the decorations scattered around Warm Springs Farm, and had been too busy to decorate her own place herself.

Biz appreciated Arthur's open-minded attitude since they were celebrating with her family at her parents' house in another country, not his own.

Simply visiting a family home in a foreign country held numerous inherent unspoken challenges.

They were the only ones staying overnight Christmas Eve at the farm with her parents. She could only hope they would get along well with all her family.

The Andrews family Christmas turned into a classic free-for-all as usual. Forced positivity turned into genuine cheerfulness over the holidays. Differences were forgiven and forgotten, and everyone appeared happy. Biz's four nieces and nephews, her younger brother's children, came for the day and pattered over the gleaming hardwood floors on their tiny feet. Some other relatives in the area visited as well.

Arthur and Biz sat in the living room by the fire for awhile before opening presents, and he spoke to her family genially. They asked him about his friends, and he said he had attended many birthday parties as a child, and still liked being a guest at parties. When her brother William's children said they wanted to watch the circus that year, referring to an annual New York extravaganza, Arthur said he would have liked to have visited a circus more often but rarely had the opportunity.

Arthur said there was much he missed since his parents had died. He did not visit his own relatives often anymore. And since he would have been completely alone for the holidays, he appreciated how the Andrews welcomed him with open arms. When the kids expressed interest during the meal in playing their video games, he offered to play with them. In short, everyone liked him.

The family planned to have Christmas dinner

early in the afternoon after they had opened presents. For a change, they had a goose dinner complete with special puddings and sauce for dessert from England, generously contributed by Arthur.

The table in the dining room had been set early, and Arthur and Biz went in to see the flower bouquets he had ordered. He smiled at Biz above the white damask tablecloth laden with sterling silver, fine bone china, and silver candlesticks as they waited in anticipation of the presents and the feast.

"I brought several gifts from England including a truly special one for you. It holds a great deal of sentimental value to me. I hope you like all of them. Let's sit in the library together a few minutes away from the others before they open presents, shall we?" he asked her quietly.

She smiled guiltily as if invited to a forbidden activity. "Sounds like a great idea to me—let's make a little escape."

They quietly made their way to the library and sat on a sofa. The room was full of the smoky aroma of the crackling aged apple tree firewood. He handed her a present he had already placed carefully on top of a stack of books.

She whistled in surprise as she accepted the present. She gently undid the wrappings and ribbons and opened the box.

The jewelry piece inside took her breath away. She instantly loved the multi-faceted oversized jewel in shiny azure tones. She made appreciative sounds, leaned over, and kissed him.

After she fondly appreciated the clear colored

brooch sparkling in the candlelight, she reached for a present to give Arthur.

He opened it, smiled, and pulled on the cardigan. "How did you know my size?"

"I found it easily enough," she said with a smile on her face. "At Collina Castle, I think, you left your sweater on a chair so I took the opportunity to check the size and ordered it online. I think the color will suit you. Burgundy looks great on you."

He took the comment well, with a smile.

"Here are a few more for you," he said warmly. He lifted a variety of boxes with ribbons, and set them next to her. He truly appeared delighted to simply give.

Feeling very lucky, she saw three gifts together on the table and joyfully opened them, one by one. He surely could not be this generous every year. She felt guilty she had not purchased more for him.

"There's more. Here's the most important present for you, stored and handed down in my family."

Biz untied the bow and ribbon on shiny crimson wrapping paper. Inside was a delicately folded lace dress. She touched the off-white cotton-lined piece of clothing gently and turned it over as she grappled to understand its significance.

"It's made of the best antique Belgian lace," he said.

She gently lifted it out of the box and looked at it, unable to speak.

Arthur turned away in a daze with a pained embarrassed expression.

"Please wait here, and I'll be back," she said and rushed away to find a room with a mirror.

"It fits," she said as she returned to show him. In fact, it was a perfect fit. A little long, perhaps, but it enhanced her curves and coloring.

"This dress is the one in the painting I made. It's actually very special and fragile as you can see." Then he paused. "My mother wore it when she was married and my grandmother as well." Without saying anymore, his eyes moistened, fearful, waiting for an answer that might tear him apart.

She gazed at him in silence, sinking and swirling softly and deeply into the spell of his endlessly radiant eyes.

They kissed for ages. When they came up for air, they gazed quietly into the fireplace together.

"My grandparents meant the world to me. They invested well, too, with an eye on conservation."

"Are you talking about the Earl of Westland?"

"Indeed, he was my grandfather," Arthur affirmed.

"I read about his tragic drowning. His yacht was caught in a severe storm on its way to Barbados. All aboard were lost at sea."

"He loved his boats, and he lived close enough to the water to breathe ocean air every day. My family's significant art collection, that he inherited, has been sold over time. A few paintings were recently delivered to me, fortunately, some of my favorite ones. My parents moved to London when they were still fairly young. After that, my grandmother sold their rather grand family house in Westland called, of course, Westland Castle."

"My grandfather had died by that time and my grandmother moved to London as well. She outlived my parents, as it turned out, since they died tragically young in a car accident. My father, an only child, would have been the heir had my grandmother died first. As you know I was his only child. When I most wanted to be a daredevil in my teens, my grandfather used to tell me I had better watch out because I was the only son of an only son four times over."

"Is that true?" Biz reacted strongly, not really intending to challenge him or expecting an answer. She was confirming her surprise at the unusual fact. The revelation made her pause and gaze at her reflection in the mirror. She knew for sure the lace dress must be extremely precious to him.

"I guess I'm feeling like a daredevil now," he said reminiscing. "He used to make me think about how lucky I am to be alive. I should be thankful just to be with you, and I am, because each and every day is a gift to me."

Chapter 41

JULIE'S TOWNHOUSE had three floors. The entrance opened onto the main floor where the living room flowed with a soaring ceiling, dining area and kitchen. Ahead a screened outdoor balcony deck had a comforting view of a scenic waterfall and a lively pond popular with ducks. Stairs descended to a media room with sofas on the floor below. And upstairs were bedrooms with another elevated outdoor deck in relative privacy.

Having collected holiday decorations from around the world for years, she decorated her Fraser fir better each year than the last one. Green and red garlands of boxwood, pine with red ribbons, and Christmas lights enlivened the atmosphere. A nook beside her staircase appeared especially charming with a miniature holly tree. Pots of poinsettia plants filled the corners and added a certain luster to the dining room where she liked to have glittery white, pink, and red plants in profusion.

The more people stand at a party in one room the better, she had heard. They stayed and talked together and that was the point. It didn't matter how large the building or house, the closer they were the friendlier guests would be to one another. She hoped her favorite friends would come because while location and food were important, exactly who actually appeared, of course, proved the single most important factor in a successful party.

She felt relieved to live close to her mother and hugged her first guest. "Happy New Year's Eve, Mom," she said with tears in her eyes.

Her green velvet dress, accented with a glamorous silver emerald necklace and bracelet set, highlighted her shiny curly brown hair. She checked her appearance one last time in the mirror, and glanced at the candlelit table as she imagined the guests would find it. Her eyes misted as she inspected an old photograph of her father framed in sterling.

When her guests arrived, they made all her hard work worthwhile when they lavishly praised the beautiful house and decorations.

Biz approved of the tree when she and Arthur arrived. She proudly introduced her guest to the hostess.

"Sorry I've been so busy lately. You might remember me mentioning Arthur visiting from England," Biz said. "Wait until you see the paintings he brought with him."

"Don't worry," said Julie, with a hug. "Thanks for coming, you two. Heavenly to see you. You're positively glowing with good health. This is Chris Newland, my colleague in California. He's originally from New Jersey. Chris, this is my old friend Biz, and her friend Arthur."

Julie felt especially pleased Chris had arrived

early to attend the party. She did not know how long her relationship with Chris would last but she had taken the risk of introducing him to her closest friends. She could not say the same had happened with her previous boyfriends. In the past, she had often kept a number of simultaneous relationships with her men friends. She could scarcely believe what was happening to her now, why she wanted to slow down, so to speak, and give her attention just to this one fellow.

"Julie has to come out to California several times in the next few months. We need her," Chris said proudly.

Julie laughed. "They need me to tell them what to do."

"Guess so. I can't exactly object to a geographical challenge," Biz said, sounding intensely happy.

Julie smiled at Arthur. "I hope you have a happy holiday and take good care of Biz. She's probably my oldest friend here in Mountain Lakes. Certainly my best."

Arthur nodded as Chris turned to speak to him.

"I heard you had a well-attended and successful show from my mother," Chris said to Arthur.

"From your mother?" asked Arthur.

"My mother owns the Newland Gallery," said Chris.

"Ah, of course! I heard your last name but what a coincidence to meet you here. Fascinating. Do you visit London often?"

"Hardly ever. Her husband is not exactly friendly to me. We don't get on well so I don't bother them. He has his own world. He doesn't invite me to accompany him to the House of Lords or the glorious stonework he inherited in Oxfordshire called Shinfold House."

"I've heard of it. That house had an airstrip left over from the Second World War," said Arthur.

When the New Year chimed in, all the guests lined up together in a circle.

"I'm so glad you all came this evening," Julie said as the partiers stayed gathered around her and Chris.

They watched the Times Square ball descend, and fireworks displayed from around the world, on a giant television screen attached to the wall. Cheering, they lifted their champagne glasses and toasted each other to a Happy New Year.

While the other guests returned to drinking and socializing, Biz and Arthur stayed glued to the TV. A reporter gave breaking news of a new art heist in Greece. It had happened only hours earlier while the owners of a priceless Renoir had gone out for the evening.

Biz found herself chilled to the bone in a way she had not been since Landon's death. For reasons she could not identify, she felt sorry for those owners. The heist on her turf in the distant country felt real to her, the threat immediate and personal. She was glad Arthur had agreed to stay on with her into the New Year and was grateful not to have to go home alone that evening.

Chapter 42

IN EARLY JANUARY the day before Arthur's scheduled return to England, he was standing outside Biz's office trying to catch her attention.

Biz was talking on the phone to Charles, the American banker she had met in Italy at Collina Castle with Arthur. Charles confirmed Signor Angelini had not been connected to the Diamondbacks, as he had guessed in Italy, and would be a trusted source for her to use in the future. Closing the conversation, she good-naturedly waved in Arthur.

He smiled and appeared in a good mood as he stepped through her door. "I suppose you heard the Diamondbacks were involved in that heist?"

"Absolutely. I heard it this morning. Someone should go there to investigate," she said.

"Could that someone possibly be me?"

She rose from her chair and walked around her desk beaming her winning smile. "Fantastic!" she said, applauding. She hugged him quickly.

"Mitch offered me a contract to help you find

out more about art heists in Greece and I wanted to tell you right away."

"I'm so pleased you persuaded him because your advice will be invaluable." Biz gave him another quick hug. "Did Mitch give you any advice when you suggested the trip?"

"Not at all. He likes you," he said, holding her around the waist.

She gazed at Arthur's face in surprise. She had not told him about Mitch.

"I'm sure Mitch wants you to be safe. He'll get a first-rate report from you," Arthur said smiling proudly. "It actually makes good business sense if I travel with you."

"I spoke to Mitch and said I was wondering if the company was doing a security check on me," she said. "I told him I saw that man with the blue hat in the driveway as proof but he assured me their security officers don't wear blue hats."

"Interesting, I wonder whether anyone's been following you. I agree, it sounds like too much of a coincidence to lose your planner, your watch, and your passport so close together. In any case, I should first return to England anyhow and meet you in Athens. I must meet with lawyers about my grandmother's estate."

"That should be fine. We need to find out whether the Diamondbacks left anything, any kind of sign, because so far the police haven't given out that level of detail. It'll be easier for us if you can advise us," she said. "And it'll be wonderful not to have to really say goodbye. At least not for long."

Chapter 43

BIZ AND HER GROUP readied themselves for their business trip to sunny Greece and were not at all sorry to escape the snowstorm forecasted for the Northeast.

On the flight itself she slept briefly, and was restless and nervous for many reasons. She very much looked forward to seeing Arthur again in a few days. With mixed pleasure, she anticipated soaking up the old world atmosphere.

Luther Banks had accompanied them in place of Landon. She still felt miserable about Landon's death and often questioned herself whether she could have done anything differently. She was beginning to wonder if Coretta would ever know who killed her husband and why. The investigation still had not made any significant progress.

On arrival they were driven from the airport into Athens by a driver wearing a uniform and a black cap with a stiff brim, and were warmly welcomed by uniformed hotel staff as they checked into their hotel.

After a brief rest, Biz sat with the others in a park-like square in Athens. She was angry and upset that her American credit card was denied when she tried to use it to pay for lunch. This was far more than embarrassing or inconvenient; it was a perilous nuisance in a foreign country. She would have to rely on the kindness of her coworkers and their shared expense account until a new card could be supplied to her. Exhausted, Biz called Dean in New Jersey remembering he had used her number for online purchases without telling her on other occasions.

"It's warm and sunny here in Athens and I'm staying at a beautiful hotel," she said.

"What exactly are you doing?" Dean asked.

"Researching the art heists."

"What's the matter? Why are you calling? I haven't heard from you in months."

She hoped he was not as hostile as his words suggested. "I might as well come right out and say it. My credit card is over its limit and I can't use it. You had access to my credit card at one time. Do you know anything about this?"

"You have so many credit cards. Why don't you just use one of the others?"

"This was the only one I brought with me. I didn't think I needed to check my account before I left because it was paid in full not long ago."

"Fine. I suppose you'll find out when the bill comes anyway. I had some unexpected expenses so I used it. "

She paused and breathed slowly, consciously wanting to end the conversation immediately, but she calmed herself down. "It really doesn't matter what you spent it on. You had no right to use my card without permission."

"I didn't really think you'd notice. I figured I'd pay you back soon enough. My job is hanging by a thread."

"I don't want anything more to do with you. That card had a twenty thousand dollar credit limit and you used it. That was wrong. I want your expenses paid off by the end of the month."

"I don't know if I can do that."

Biz found her hands shaking. "Do you know your actions have left me in Europe without a credit card that works?"

"So what? You should have brought two. Your company has a basically bottomless expense account. And it won't kill you if you can't shop every minute."

"Take care of this," she said in a low measured voice knowing her anger was about to rise beyond her control. "I'm busy and I have to go now."

Walking around the park in front of the others, she wondered if he had ever really cared about her or respected her. The upsetting conversation rattled her because it signaled the final end of their long friendship. She could feel it. And she wondered whether she would ever get the money back he had taken from her.

Chapter 44

JESSIE, GINA, AND LUTHER watched Biz pacing just out of hearing distance. A grey tabby cat walked past and brushed against Biz's leg as if to comfort her but Biz did not seem to notice. From the sound of her voice she had been having a heated discussion.

When Biz walked back to them, she briefly explained the reason for her declined credit card. Embarrassed, she told them quite honestly she felt like being alone. After accompanying her back to the hotel, they departed on their shopping excursions. She would have to pay off the twenty thousand or her credit rating would plummet. She could transfer the funds from a savings account but the process might take a few days of discomfort. Until then, she would have to make do with the company's expense account for meals. Luckily, the others had company cards. Biz loved to shop but she could live without it. What bothered her was feeling helpless and victimized by someone she had cared about.

Alone, she reclined on her sumptuous bed, arranged some brocade tasseled pillows around her, and lapsed into tears. She fell further into despair as old feelings of victimization by men kept pushing their way to the surface. Unhappy memories of her miscarriage rose again unbidden. Mitch had not wanted her. Dean had not truly loved her. Even her position at the television of which she felt so proud would one day finish.

She yearned to escape to a peaceful place in her mind, a symbol of security for her. An image of her family's land with the sandy beach near Ottawa drifted into her mind. She just wished she could lie down on the beach that second and listen to gentle waves wash onto the shore on a warm summer day.

Gradually, she did not feel alone but as if another person had joined her and was present in the room with her. The presence that remained with her cared deeply about her and guided her thoughts to a gentler place away from any emotional pain she could inflict on herself.

It had happened to her before, especially in moments of deepest despair like this. She recognized the presence of the Higher Being, the only one who could ultimately provide her with peace to save her inner soul. She recognized this as a universal emotion she liked to call God.

She felt the presence leading her mind to feelings of compassion for herself and others. Accompanying more peaceful thoughts, she mercifully found the calmness she craved in gentle clouds of sleepy oblivion.

Chapter 45

A FEW HOURS later Biz awoke from her nap refreshed with renewed strength. A swim in the hotel pool would do her good before dinner. First, she roused herself enough to check American business news.

Arthur had recommended to her the shares of a certain brand of paints that he insisted were the best in the world for oil paintings. The shares had just begun to trade in America in an initial public offering. Not a secret at all, she had reported the story herself and snapped up some shares. That same afternoon the market ascended quickly, and her stocks astounded her. Her paint stock exploded in price, from a couple of dollars a share to thirty dollars, as it traded in New York. She sat back in awe. The amount she had gained in one day was exactly twenty thousand.

Beholding her good fortune with a measure of disbelief, she texted Arthur right away to thank him for his advice. She was proud of choosing two winners and promptly paid her credit card bill with a light heart. At minimum, this task had been properly done.

Biz met her coworkers the next morning to visit art museums for business. She would have liked to share the excursion with Arthur except that he had not arrived. He had been delayed in England and intended to fly to Athens as soon as he could, perhaps the next day. That meeting he had planned with his lawyers in London concerning his grandmother's estate had been especially urgent. Time without him would give Biz a chance to finish news reports and further investigate a theft at a major museum.

They sat outside in the sun in Athens, and had a late afternoon break at a restaurant surrounded by golden-colored stucco buildings. Relaxing on its' spacious terrace, they appreciated strong, black coffee served in thick white porcelain cups and saucers. Knowing it had snowed in New Jersey, the team felt lucky to have escaped the worst snowstorm in thirty years. They cooperated smoothly, clearly in high spirits.

They liked having Luther as cameraman on this trip and welcomed his advice, since he had worked well with them in New York for years. Biz especially respected his education from a good school, as she had with Landon.

Needing a pen, Biz searched all around her chair anxiously, and blurted out, "My handbag…Where is it?"

"It was hanging from your chair," said Luther helpfully, otherwise at a total loss.

"Could you please help me find it?" asked Biz.

The others immediately wanted to help to allay her rising sense of panic. They stood up, searched the vicinity of the table and briefly asked other customers and the wait staff. They could not find it anywhere.

"I'm sorry. I can't even remember seeing you carrying it," said Gina solicitously. "Maybe you forgot it at the hotel. What did you have in it that you would miss besides your ID?"

Biz glanced at Gina and squinted in the sun. "I can hardly see you, the sun is so bright here. I think my bag had my wallet, ticket information, and maybe my passport."

"We have to report this right away," said Luther.

Biz left them in a hurry and rushed the short block to the hotel by herself through the center of Athens. Maybe I'm paranoid, she thought. First, the cell phone was misplaced, her planner was lost, and after that, a man possibly stalked her in New Jersey. Then, her watch and passport had disappeared, and now her crocodile handbag had been stolen in broad daylight. What a run of bad luck. She had, as it happened, intended to replace it. Luckily, it was not one of her new ones from Paris. Who would want to steal an old handbag, she wondered.

Fortunately, her cell phone rested safely in her pocket. She called Arthur for sympathy as she walked into her hotel. By chance, she had kept her keys in her pocket.

"I was going to call you today, so I'm glad you called when you had a chance," he said, soothingly. "How're things going?"

"You'll never believe what's just happened!" she said breathlessly, grateful to hear his calming voice. "My handbag's been stolen. It had nearly everything, my cards and all. Fortunately, I left my passport in my suitcase this time."

"That's a pity. Did anyone hurt you?" He sounded more concerned about her personal safety and wellbeing than the loss, which she appreciated.

"No, it wasn't violent at all. I suppose it could have been worse. One moment I had my handbag and a few moments later I didn't have it. It was almost like magic, the way it disappeared so quickly."

"If it was done so unobtrusively," said Arthur, "it was probably done by an expert who knew what he was doing. It's not your fault."

"Thanks. Don't worry, I'll take care of it myself. When are you coming?" she said.

"I won't take long. I finished everything I needed to do with my grandmother's estate. I'll fly to Athens early tomorrow," he said.

"I can't wait to see you again."

"Just try to make it through tonight."

Another lesson she learned from the experience: be careful when traveling not to carry all essential cards at once, and carry extras. She could eventually replace her driver's license and credit card but it would take time.

She felt momentary panic, all alone, vulnerable, and anxious about the possibility of identity theft. If only Arthur were with her instead of being in England. Yet she knew in his heart he cared about her, and she felt comforted by the thought. She could handle it.

Chapter 46

BIZ MET HER GROUP in the lobby to take a cab out for a late dinner after she had another swim. They enjoyed walking around at night in Athens. There were always other people around, and stores usually stayed open late.

As planned, they met Julie and Chris that evening in the lobby before going out for dinner. They hugged one another in greeting. The couple appeared in good spirits after their trip around Greece.

Biz kept her spirits up for them despite her apprehensions. She explained her plight after losing her handbag. While comforted with their sympathy, she preferred to focus on them rather than her own problems.

"Greece is magical, isn't it? Have you enjoyed your trip so far?" asked Biz.

"Of course," her friend said. "We boarded a ferry to take us to the island of Mykonos but the Aegean Sea became wickedly rough. We left at the next landing and happened on the sparsely inhabited island of Tinos. We enjoyed visiting the beaches and villages for a few days before we hopped across the water to Mykonos. The windmills and the white-washed houses were beautiful in the sun. It was great fun to sit on a balcony and enjoy the sunsets for a few days. All in all, it's been a fabulous holiday."

"I'm totally happy for both of you," said Biz. "You're so lucky. It's a beautiful country; I'll probably wish I could stay longer."

Biz gazed around the lobby, and momentarily focused on a vaguely familiar swarthy man with a camera. She could swear she remembered him as the same photographer in Italy that Landon had remarked on. She began to shake as she remembered what happened to Landon, but when she skimmed the crowd to find him a second time, he had disappeared.

"You're shaking," said Julie concerned. "What's the matter? Have you seen a ghost?"

"I don't know," Biz chattered. "Maybe I did. A local photographer took pictures of us in Rome, and I think he was just here in this room. Landon promised to call the office about him, and remember what happened to him? The man I just saw looked like the same individual but when I turned around, he'd vanished."

"Are you sure?" asked Julie.

"I can't see him now. There's nothing I can do here except to keep watching for him, and be ready to run. I can't involve the police because he melts into the crowds here. Anyway, don't worry about me. My coworkers have plans to sightsee tomorrow morning and perhaps you could join us. We'd like to visit the Acropolis and have lunch at a restaurant located at the tip-top of Mount Lycabettus with an incredible view. Sounds ambitious to do both but we could." She did not want Julie and Chris to have any reason to beg off the invitation. "Please come with us?"

Julie turned to Chris and talked to him quietly for just a few seconds and appeared rather puzzled.

"We've already been to the Acropolis and it's a long walk but coincidentally we also made plans to meet Chris's stepfather for lunch at the restaurant on Mount Lycabettus."

"Turns out, I'm meeting Lord Dawson at lunch, too. I need to question him about his deals. He must have double-booked himself," she affirmed, referring to the short interview she had scheduled. "We can have a horse-drawn carriage ride to the top of the Acropolis and then meet him. Please come with me," she pleaded. "I love carriage rides and can't wait to have one this trip."

"Maybe. We had to be patient when we rode mules on the islands but it was great fun," Julie said and smiled. She had enjoyed the change from her modern fast-paced professional life to this dramatically slower pace. "On the other hand, it might be fun to ascend the Acropolis one more time in a carriage. It sure was a hike!" She glanced at Chris to gain his approval.

"Hey, maybe with a ride, we'll go," Chris chimed in and gazed at Julie, who smiled.

"We'll do both," said Biz.

"In that case, you're on," said Julie.

"I'll probably have to owe you for the ride but I'll pay you back as soon as I can I promise."

"That's what friends are for," said Julie warmly.

Biz awoke early the next day, researched the financial report she had to write, and reviewed questions she would ask Lord Dawson at lunch. She also tried to make more calls to correct her credit in the aftermath of her handbag theft.

She felt alone, and thought of Arthur any time she had a moment to reflect. She liked him very much now and wanted to have more time with him. Their relationship had become considerably more serious, and she felt sure he would have comforted and helped with her challenges in Athens. They would soon be together.

At ten in the morning, the group began the ascent to the full height of the Acropolis. Jessie, Gina, and Luther planned to walk up and down the mountain at their own speed and find their own rides. In the horse-drawn carriage with Julie and Chris, Biz thought Julie had done well to choose the computer genius and liked him. He was good with women and charmed her with his random complimentary comments. For some reason, perhaps because he was so responsive, she assumed he had a close relationship with his mother.

Awesome late-morning views of the city and the ruins dazzled the trio as the carriage wound its way up the curvy stone lane to the ancient summit of the Acropolis.

"This ancient amphitheater built into the mountainside is fit for a king, isn't it?" Chris said.

Julie mused, "I love the honey color of these ancient rocks."

Colorful natural beauty harmonized well with important archeological and architectural vistas. They were deeply impressed as they took numerous photos to record their journey.

When they attained the top of the Acropolis, they climbed ancient steps and followed walkways from one end of the enormous structure to the other. Gigantic rectangular stones dated back millennia. Parched rocks shimmered in bright sunlight until they appeared moist and alive, as if they could breathe. If only humans could understand them.

Modern day visitors could easily imagine traveling back in time in this historic setting. They could have stood there thousands of years before and watched the same awe-inspiring views. Seeing the new museum of statues and artifacts would have been time well-spent but they did not have much time and had to leave soon to have lunch.

Biz walked around huge ruins of statues, lintels and columns of stone feeling hugely adventurous and carefree at that altitude high above the city. Mount Lycabettus perched at the highest point in the shimmering distance. She could breathe in the fresh air deeply, smell fragrant pine trees, and watch them waving in the evanescent breeze. Her spirits recovered and she felt much happier and stronger. Soon she would have her money and her passport, and everything would be fine.

When they finished their tour of the Acropolis, they descended by foot. A taxi Biz had reserved awaited them. The taxi stopped at the hotel for Biz before whisking Julie and Chris away through the ancient hills to Mount Lycabettus. She planned to go on ahead to the restaurant later with her coworkers, after a quick stop at the hotel for some essentials she needed to conduct the interview.

To reach the restaurant, they would have to take a tram the last few hundred feet straight up the side of a cliff. The restaurant at the apex of Mount Lycabettus where they planned to meet again promised to have a beautiful view of the city surrounding Athens, and placed it firmly among the most magnificent views in the region on anyone's list.

Biz thought ahead to the brief interview she planned to have with Lord Dawson. She had talked to him in Oxford and persuaded him to meet them while in Athens on business. As she walked into the hotel expecting to meet her coworkers, she could hardly wait to leave with them and have lunch. The time approached two o'clock.

At the front desk of the hotel she asked for her keys. They had asked her to turn them in the same morning and she had done so without questioning the reason. She assumed they wanted the keys for mysterious foreign legal purposes, perhaps to assert their ownership.

"May I please have my room keys?" she asked.

"Your name?" asked the uniformed man at the front desk.

"Andrews, Biz," she said, somewhat impatiently. She wanted to rush out again as soon as she located the papers.

"I see nothing here for you," he said casually in her direction. He appeared vaguely familiar and wore a uniform and a hat but from where she stood, she did not recognize him.

Her world began to sway as she realized she must have forgotten to check that her reservation was not cancelled when she was asked to turn in her keys.

"I don't understand. I've been staying here for the last few days."

"Your reservation ended this morning. Someone else has already taken your room and we have no other rooms available."

"That's impossible." She panicked when she remembered that she had left her clothes in her suitcases. "Where are my suitcases? Where are my clothes?"

"I will look for them if you will wait here, please," he said as he walked into the room behind him.

Her belongings were evidently removed from her room without her authority. A sickening feeling hit her when she remembered she had left her passport inside a suitcase rather than her handbag, another reason she needed to have her suitcase. She still did not have any identification on her after losing her handbag on the plaza. Inside her pocket she did not have enough money to take a cab to the restaurant to meet the others. She had been in a hurry, depending on the kindness of her teammates to handle those details.

"I'm sorry," the front desk attendant said mournfully when he came back. "Your suitcases are not here. You will have to file a police report, one for every suitcase."

Something in her said this was not right; the attendant denied her key request too easily. It had happened so fast and so casually. But then her panic buried the feeling.

"It will take awhile," he continued in his Greek accent. "Don't worry, I will take you there. It is a law in our country. Any theft must be reported to a police station."

She moaned. This would be a major inconvenience. She was already late and in a hurry to do the interview. She was surprised the team was not here waiting for her.

A few minutes later, she stood outside the hotel. She saw an official public vehicle pull over to the curb. At the same time, the hotel doorman motioned to her. She walked out the door in a daze to meet the same uniformed man in a hat from the front desk. He ushered her into the backseat of a car. He pulled it out onto the street and his face looked at hers in the rearview mirror.

At that moment, behind what must have been a fake mustache and a wig of wavy dark hair, she recognized the face of the uniformed hotel clerk from another time and place. She tried hard to open the door to leave the vehicle at a stoplight but it was centrally locked and she could not make it open. She was caught and she knew it.

Chapter 47

JULIE AND CHRIS patiently waited for Biz to appear inside the restaurant and admired the stunning view. The mountaintop itself had been an adventure to reach. After their taxi halted, they had ascended on the inclined rail car. The ride up the steep side of the mountain had given them gorgeous views of the city and the Mediterranean Sea.

They had arranged to meet Lord Dawson in the entry hall of the restaurant. They waited patiently and had not requested to be seated in case Lord Dawson had a strong seating preference.

Jessie, Gina, and Luther were waiting for him there, and for Biz as well. Lord Dawson had asked them to meet him early at the restaurant and they had not been able to find Biz to tell her. Julie mentioned that Biz had expected to meet them at the hotel and they were all concerned.

Chris's stepfather arrived late and ashen-faced, looking ill and haggard.

"Come in and sit down," said Lord Dawson forcefully. "I have to make an important announcement that will concern and unfortunately inconvenience everyone in the entire restaurant."

Chris turned in evident dismay to Julie. He was annoyed not to be given time to properly introduce her to his strong-willed stepfather.

Lord Dawson took it upon himself to ask to speak to the management of the restaurant, and held a cordless microphone Luther happened to hand to him. As if entitled to make any announcement he liked, he rose with some self-importance to speak to his audience.

"Excuse me. I have a vital announcement to make that may save your life," he proclaimed to the entire room of diners. And they were certainly startled to be alerted in this way. "A large stray long-haired black dog, perhaps wild, is roaming outside the restaurant at this very moment. You must not leave the building. This dog exhibits clear signs of rabies. I am only telling you this for your own protection. The police have been alerted. I repeat that I strongly advise you not to leave the restaurant under any circumstances until the animal has been captured and removed. We will tell you when it's safe to leave the building. Thank you."

Patrons of the restaurant smiled politely. Nodding their heads in grateful agreement, they continued to dine amidst sumptuous surroundings, thick white tablecloths, and clinking glassware.

Chapter 48

BIZ SAT IN a pronounced state of shock in the back seat of the taxi. She could see Stewart focusing his unblinking gaze on her in the mirror. Driving erratically, he stared aggressively straight into her eyes as often as he could.

She felt inside her pocket. Her fingers found her cell phone. It was low on battery but at least it was there. Luckily, she had Arthur's number handy in her phone log. She pressed speed dial and hoped he would know enough to listen and keep on listening.

"Stewart, is that you?" she said out loud to the driver.

Clearly not in any mood to converse, he pulled the car into the busy lanes of traffic. He had not heard Arthur answer quietly, although Biz had. They were delayed temporarily by stoplights and traffic but she could not escape the locked car.

Then he raised his voice and intoned with menacing anger, "You'll find everything will be easier for you if you keep quiet."

His accent sounded different. In surprise, she said, "You're American."

"My name was Vince Terrino when I lived there."

His answer shocked and rendered her speechless as she contemplated her situation. He had been an easy-going fellow in England with his British accent. He had opened her eyes to sights in Oxford and London that she might not have noticed without his advice. Yet she was still surprised he had appeared in front of her without a word of warning in Rome, shaking like a drug addict.

As they picked up speed and drove close to the top of Mount Lycabettus, the view, heightened by her fears, took her breath away. She could see along the rooftops of the city as far as the Mediterranean Sea. The car pulled to an abrupt halt in a dusty square of cleared land. Biz saw, to her dismay, the sandy lot appeared completely empty. Dry dust swirled in circles.

In the rearview mirror, Stewart's eyes smoldered like a forest fire. He stopped the car so it became hidden.

"Now get out," he said roughly.

He walked her on to a platform of gravel overlooking a rocky ravine. Far above the city, he took her arm more roughly and jolted her almost off her feet in a surprisingly angry and violent way.

No one seemed anywhere near them. Biz could see apartment buildings further on down and she could hear filtered sounds of traffic and honking horns. They were only expressions of normal life but she clung to them from within the unreal situation.

She would have to persuade this violent man

who turned out to be psychopathic not to kill her. In a moment of sheer terror, she faced the horrific question of how many murderers had identities truthfully known only to their victims.

"What are you doing, Stewart? Or should I call you Vince?"

"I've been following you. That's what I've been doing," he said.

"Why would you do that?" she asked, and her voice sounded different to herself, far away and small. She could only think of questions to ask him.

"It's not really you I have a grudge against. Although it's not exactly easy to like people like you. Hell no, it's your father. He destroyed my life. Took my family away. Took everything away by putting me in prison."

"My father is a lawyer. It's the jury that convicts, not the prosecution."

"He argued that I was lot higher up, a lot more influential than I was. I was put in jail and all the legal work against me had been finished. It was obvious your father was going to make me serve a lot of time in prison. I was going to get thirty to life. That means life. That means I never see my kids grow up and when I get out, my beautiful wife is seventy years old."

"Did you…did you kill Landon?"

"I used to work at WYN-TV. I was a cameraman, just like your friend Landon."

"Did you kill him?" she repeated, nearly screaming.

"He was the only person who might have recognized me from back in the day. So yeah, when I got a chance, I killed him. My bracelet got left behind. No sweat."

Tears streamed down Biz's cheeks as Vince continued speaking almost conversationally, "The way I see it, I put that guy out of his misery. They pay the cameramen nothing. Not like the hot shot salaries they pay the on air talent, as they say. They're all just like you. They show up with a push up bra and read off a cue card and suddenly they're making twelve times my salary. I had to find a second job on the side." He lifted his hand and showed her his ring with the symbolic crest of the syndicate on it.

"My father told me it was unthinkable he, I mean you, would still be alive. Everyone on that boat was presumed lost at sea."

"They didn't ever find out the truth, did they?" Stewart laughed. "Good."

He gulped sandy air and grabbed her arm angrily, took some rope from his car, and bound her legs and arms as she screamed. As he sat and surveyed his handiwork, he held out a towel he intended to use as a gag.

"You'd better keep quiet or I'll use this and you won't be able to say anything. You might not be able to breathe either," he said nastily.

The knots seemed to tighten themselves the more she struggled. She could not escape. And she couldn't reach her pocket to tell if Arthur had picked up the call or not.

"When I get done with you, no one will recognize you, let alone connect you with me," he said. He spat and continued, "Both of them are my enemies and I can get to them where they will both hurt. That would be through you. My motivation is to hurt them. I'm a free man now and I owe my buddies the Diamondbacks. They came for me. Put me on a boat and a plane out of the States." He coughed a nervous hollow sound.

Biz stared at him, terrified. "You're not free. Besides, what use am I to the Diamondbacks?"

She decided she would use the truth as her weapon, and kept engaging him with comments that would make him keep talking.

"You're too curious. You might find out too much so they want you to get your nose out of the business."

"Everything about your life is a lie," Biz said. "Even how you look."

"Doesn't mean I'm not free. I looked different in the States and I sounded different, too. Now that I'm living in Europe, my nose is straighter and my hair color is black, not light brown. I grew a beard and mustache. I lost a lot of weight and took on a different style of clothes and shoes. I wanted to look completely different, more dignified, so I could meet the kind of people who collect art. In fact, I was in the U.S. scheduled for laser surgery so I wouldn't have to wear glasses anymore, and that's when I first followed you. Do you recognize this?"

He replaced the uniform cap he had on with a blue baseball hat from his pocket and smirked knowingly as he put it on. His metal ring sharply flashed the crest of the Diamondbacks in the sunlight.

She finally knew for certain, he was the one who had been in the car on the driveway at Warm Springs Farm.

He tied a scarf around his face to protect himself. Thick clouds of sand blew swirling around them at this impressive height in a sharp wind. Then he maneuvered her just inside the entrance of a small cave overlooking a cliff. She heard his words muffled as if through a blanket.

"That's right," he continued, reading her expression. "I was all over following you. I saw everything. I was looking through the window of your house, too, when your friend turned over the painting in your living room."

"I remember that," Biz said, barely able to breathe. Her captor's ring had a DB logo or crest on it just like the one on her painting. She visibly shook and her muscles ached where the rope uncomfortably chafed her skin.

"And the recent art heists, were you a part of those?"

She tried to distract this madman, fascinated and horrified at the deadly game he was playing. At the same time, the reporter in her wanted to hear all the angles. She thought she would deserve a Pulitzer if she lived to tell about what she learned now, firsthand, about the Diamondbacks.

"We just took the paintings we could get and sold them as if they were fakes but we left our crest on them if we did. Sometimes we'd take the paintings around the world and sell them to fabulously wealthy people in far away countries for lots of money," he said, smiling at the memory. "Maybe you were lucky and your painting is a genuine masterpiece but it doesn't matter because you're never going to see it again."

"You disgust me." She sputtered the words but they were drowned in the wind.

The two of them were isolated at the far end of a totally empty, horrifically sandy clearing surrounded by enormous ancient boulders.

She guessed the others were waiting at the

restaurant in relatively close proximity also at the top of Mount Lycabettus, but far enough away they would never hear her screams. She became inert without the use of her limbs, bound and useless as they were. Her throat had grown dry and she coughed hollowly in the dry sandy atmosphere, almost unable to see anything. With the fear, the altitude, and the pressure of the ropes on her bones, she gagged, almost sick to her stomach.

"Come here," he said angrily as he motioned her to crawl from the cave onto a bench with her back to a cliff behind it. "If I pushed you off this cliff, no one would ever suspect me."

Her heart raced. She would have to think quickly. No one would be likely to pass close enough, have sufficient courage, reflexes, and presence of mind to instantly rescue her even if they could see her. She felt trapped, all alone with this wild acquaintance who raged like a madman. She was about to fall backwards into the abyss. No one would be wise enough to say Stewart had pushed her. Even if questioned by the police, and that was unlikely, he might say she had fallen instead of confessing he had any part of it.

She looked at him with an overwhelming sense of fear as she thought he might actually do it. She felt unsure how to handle him the next few moments. But without any doubt they were absolutely key to her survival.

"What are you going to do to me?"

"Whatever I want. I can do what I want, go where I want, and I will never be caught. We get away with all kinds of things. Vince Terrino is dead. And Stewart, Lord Dawson's driver, is a nice man who lives in England." He pointed his arm over the cliff with a wild glint in his eye. "They'd think you just went for a short walk by yourself and fell off this wall. And it's a long way down."

She tried to scream but he pushed her closer to the edge every time.

"I haven't done anything to hurt you. I even thought you liked me."

"You thought," he said contemptuously. "You thought."

He quickly withdrew a knife from his belt and held it to her chin.

"Your father must be punished. He takes my children from me. I take his child from him." Stewart began to walk around waving his knife, wildly out of control.

Looking down in shocked desperation at the spellbinding panoramic view of the city below, she tried to reason with him. Her thoughts raced madly. She knew she was playing with fire but she wanted to tell him the truth and keep him talking to her, to buy herself more time. Where are my friends when I need them, she silently agonized. She stretched her muscles and pulled her arms and legs to escape.

"It sounds to me as if you're the one who brought all this on yourself when you joined the syndicate," she said. "You can't expect to break the law again and again, and not get caught."

Vince reared up at her comment as if to attack her.

At the same time, she just barely detected a human form walking toward them out of the corner of her eye.

Chapter 49

THE TALL GAUNT male figure continued to walk slowly toward them until he stopped a short distance away.

Vince backed off when he noticed the distinguished-looking man.

Immediately, hoping she was saved, Biz called out. "Help me, Lord Dawson. Please untie me. He's crazy and he's going to kill me."

Not in the least frightened, the older man looked at her in silence but did not attempt to rescue her. He sauntered to the pair slowly until he stood in front of them.

"Help me!" Biz repeated, shocked at his inaction.

"Do it," Lord Dawson finally said to Stewart.

Instead of untying her, Stewart casually wrapped a blue and white paisley bandana around his index finger and stuffed it in her mouth as she screamed and pleaded.

Biz watched helplessly as the two men turned to face each other and exchanged congenial greetings. All the while they kept flashing rings bearing the Diamondbacks insignia.

She had a better idea now of Lord Dawson's loyalties, and of who and what he really was.

Chapter 50

AFTER A FEW MINUTES passed, Stewart advanced on Biz. He looked ready to drag her to the cliff's edge.

"Do it," Lord Dawson repeated, to encourage him to push her over the abyss.

Her time was running out. Her beating heart lurched again first with fear. And then suddenly with joy. Could she be hallucinating from fear?

Her sweetheart Arthur appeared, rushing into the small parking area. Along with him was a casually dressed man who looked vaguely familiar and carried a camera.

Lord Dawson swung around to face them. Stewart further tightened his grip on her arm and held her sharply as if in a clamp.

The photographer set down his camera quickly and drew a gun on her captor and the older man. "I'm a sharp shooter," he said in warning.

Tensing his teeth, Stewart glared at them with hot rage, then spat. "Take one step closer and she goes over the edge!" He pushed her closer to the precipice. The edge approached her at close range but Biz struggled to stay as far away as she could from the precipice. Leaning over backward, she let out a squeak of fear.

Arthur could have offered some resistance. Instead, he immediately retreated, and made a quick decision to play along. "I can write you a money order right now. You can take it and leave. We won't follow you. Just don't hurt her."

Biz continued to weep, and gave muffled moans of panic as Stewart pushed her further out toward the cliff.

The photographer aimed his gun at Stewart.

Suddenly Arthur went charging at Lord Dawson, wrestling him to the ground cold.

The spectacle surprised Stewart just long enough to pause and look around. The sharp shooter took careful aim and put a bullet in Stewart's leg. Stewart fell unconscious into the sand.

Chapter 51

HEARING THE COMMOTION, Chris Newland
walked in their direction from the deck of the
restaurant above them. He increased his speed as he
approached the unexpected and noisy spectacle
around the corner. Despite being surprised, he
reacted quickly, turned around, and rushed back
into the restaurant to alert the police and restaurant
staff.

Fortunately, the police were already in the
vicinity since, unknown to Lord Dawson, the
restaurant had telephoned them to take care of an
incident concerning a rabid dog. Of course, there
was not a single dog to be found. Lord Dawson had
used the announcement he had made to buy Stewart
the time and privacy he needed. And in the end it
had backfired. The police were already on their way
to the scene to help locate the dangerous canine.

Several emergency responders, mostly waiters,
rushed out to help. The police arrived and quickly
assessed the scene. They bound Stewart with a rope
in case he tried to escape. But that was unlikely

since he had fainted from a loss of blood and required medical care.

An ambulance arrived and removed the bloodied kidnapper, and police officers took Lord Dawson away to jail.

In relief, Biz fell into Arthur's arms. Her tension broke and she began to weep.

After a tearful and wordless minute, she reached in her pocket and pulled out her cell phone. The battery was dead.

"How did you find me?"

"You were very helpful when you dialed my number in the car. I could hear from the tone of your voice that something was wrong. But I couldn't figure out where you were. Thank goodness Stewart is a talker. It bought us both time. Mitch told me, back when I was in the States, he'd been worried you were being followed and installed a special tracker on your cell phone that gave me your exact geographical coordinates. Worked even when your battery went out. In fact, it was especially useful when the phone didn't work. We weren't sure if Stewart had found it. It was risky. I'm truly sorry it took far too long for us to find you on the mountain. I'll always have trouble forgiving myself for not being with you when you needed me."

"You were, though." Biz looked at him, dazed.

"I suppose it's major news for you then that Lord Dawson is the founder of the Diamondbacks," said Arthur. "Was news for me, too, until just a little while ago."

"So much for his integrity; he made those inside traders in New York seem like small fries."

"He even had a connection to those inside traders at Weston & Marks in London and should have been caught for his involvement in that as well. Don't worry, without any doubt, he'll have to be imprisoned, and so will Stewart." Arthur kissed her.

"I can't believe I didn't know," Biz said, still wiping her eyes with her sleeve.

Then the photographer walked over to them and introduced himself as Tony. Arthur said Tony had been trailing Stewart for a while and was hired by WYN-TV. Apparently Landon had called and checked the station from Rome, and been reassured about Tony. As it turned out, Biz had not ever been informed and alerted by design. Mitch did not want to scare her until they knew for certain some scheme that might endanger her was really going on.

And that almost got me killed, Biz thought, but decided to let it go for now.

"We finally joined the dots," continued Arthur, later in the car. "We found Lord Dawson played a major role as head of the Diamondbacks. The police recently discovered the headquarters of the organization on the estate in the Cotswolds, and I had to see it. I did finish some work on my grandmother's estate while I visited England but when the police requested my assistance to help inspect Shinfold House, I was shocked at what we found."

Biz had been advised, as a matter of strict secrecy, that Morris, Inc. had been working covertly for over fifteen years on national security issues. She already knew Arthur had a critical interest in her security, which she had simply chalked up to his romantic interest in her. She had not suspected any wider interests in security issues of international organizations beyond art thefts that Arthur evidently had.

"I've had Stewart, as you call him, followed and investigated. I also read about his history from a background check. He hasn't been honest with you from the beginning and obviously he has been known by another name. Morris, Inc. has been very helpful and performed a thorough international investigation aided by computer cryptography and law enforcement authorities.

"Neither of them were the kind of people you would want to have anything to do with. Stewart or Vince joined the Diamondbacks and was almost imprisoned by your father except he escaped. He even took your favorite watch to a pawn shop. Tony, our driver, was a private detective and a sharp shooter hired by the station to double as a photographer. He followed Stewart and even bought your watch back for you."

"My watch?" She thought sadly of the timepiece she had given up as lost.

Her whole body still shook as she recovered from her trauma. For some reason, having her watch returned to her, from the security that had been following her without her knowing, drove home to her how helpless she had been.

"Are you angry?" he asked, aware of her expression.

"Why did they follow me without giving me a word to warn me? How could they do that? That was a serious invasion of my privacy. They should have warned me," she said.

"The station wanted you to have higher

security clearance level to take on more difficult stories. Mitch was secretly working with the government and testing an especially durable cell phone tracker developed by a company he bought. That cell phone was the device that helped us find you. I, for one, am glad they were concerned with your security, and the tracker worked so we could find you. I was grateful for their assistance. You probably would have been killed if Tony and I hadn't found you. Mitch told Tony to pick me up at the airport and we drove straight here. They both suspected and agreed with me that something had gone wrong and we had to find you.

"The Diamondbacks expanded into Europe and made new contacts. They were involved in a number of illicit activities. They've been found responsible for art thefts, bribery, fake passports and visas, smuggling and gambling interests. They used wine bottles to smuggle liquid dope, which is why they wanted to learn more about your story, how much you had learned about the organization, and what you would talk about in your reports. We simply didn't know then as much as we know now about the Diamondbacks. Stewart was an evil guy responsible to a bad crowd for his life of freedom overseas."

"I only wish you had warned me a long time ago and not left me in the dark," she said. "Stewart and I just had an innocent business relationship. I had barely met the man, and I didn't have any idea he could be dangerous."

"We didn't either, believe me, or we would have warned you. There's more we found out about him," Arthur said. "His name was actually Vince Terrino in America before he changed it."

"He told me," she said. "He was a thief who owed his life to the Diamondbacks. He wasn't a driver for Lord Dawson in England for decades as it appeared."

"Exactly. It was just a hunch but when he went to Italy and Greece we followed him, except we unfortunately missed his attack on Landon. After that, I investigated it further for you; that's another reason to explain why I'm here. The station helped fund the security aspect. At every point you were well-covered.

"Mitch told me that before he was killed, Landon telephoned the station and verified the identity of the photographer in Italy, and found out he was legitimately with security. Landon, and in Greece, Luther, didn't worry because Tony followed you more than Vince or Stewart did," said Arthur. "You're extremely important to the company, and they hope you can do more advanced work for them. That's why Tony followed the group inconspicuously. There's no need to fret. I'm sorry I couldn't tell you. The company warned me I had to keep it quiet."

"What gave you the confidence to bring down Lord Dawson?" she asked.

"I'd learned basic wrestling moves but I hadn't ever used them like that before."

She glanced at him with surprise. It was true then after all. She had not simply imagined she had been followed again and again in Europe. As angry, shocked, and conflicted as she was, one mystery had been solved to her satisfaction. The reason her stalker had been followed was that the station had begun to be concerned after she had run into a string of bad luck. She had to change her attitude and be relieved and grateful the company had watched out for her as a sort of professional responsibility. It had clearly surpassed any security protection the company had been obligated to provide.

She wondered why she had not strung together certain clues. Stewart, or Vince, had appeared in Rome unannounced in a country three hours by plane away from England. She had briefly suspected he might have stolen her passport but she had not followed through on it. The worst part of all was that he had schemed to cause trouble and followed her primarily to disrupt her investigation. He wanted to harm her father and even Mitch Morris and WYN-TV by killing her.

A female physician came to the hotel, examined and treated her for superficial wounds, and cleared her to travel. The physical wounds she had would take time to heal. But the emotional shock of the incident where she had been personally targeted would take far longer.

Arthur stayed with her since she asked him to stay and felt safer with him around. He gently helped Biz bathe away all signs of the filthy incident and made phone calls about outgoing jet flights. He felt especially sorry about how long it had taken to find and rescue her, and said her pain hurt him almost as much.

Biz felt extremely lucky to be alive and needed time to rest and recuperate.

Chapter 52

AS BIZ AND ARTHUR wound down from the unexpectedly dangerous episode and the news spread, job offers from rival television stations came pouring in. So far, she had given rival offers little consideration but her most recent experience as a journalist, combined with her new relationship with Arthur, motivated her to contemplate a change. Having confronted certain unsettled priorities regarding her job at WYN-TV, her recovery time offered her the opportunity to think and plan her future.

Meanwhile, Lord Dawson's arrest brought important information to light. His fellow lords and banker associates had not had any inkling of his activities during his extended weekend visits to his estate.

To fund his secret organization, he had started a scheme forty years earlier. He had embezzled funds from clients who had died without wills and did not have survivors who might sue for claims. With seed profits from a secret scheme he devised, he started a hedge fund from the proceeds. He made astounding returns for his private clients and returned an exorbitant percentage of the large profits assumed to be from investments. He shamed his investors into staying in the fund, remained very secretive about publishing yield numbers, and creatively deployed their funds for his own use.

With his replenished family fortune, he founded the Diamondbacks. The organization smuggled everything from drugs, firearms, art, and jewelry heists to passports and visas, and sold them around the globe. If money could be made, they wanted their share. This business, which he still regarded as private, had grown into a worldwide web of associates and he profited from their low-paid labor.

Lord Dawson falsely assured almost everyone, even his wives, that the land on which his outbuildings stood, entered by a separate driveway, belonged to the county. As landowner, he simply walked past a hedge to his headquarters to conveniently pursue his clandestine activities.

On the grounds of Shinfold House, he built a high-tech headquarters and outfitted his buildings with state-of-the-art electronics, television screens, computer screens, and fiber-optic wireless boosts for lightning-fast internet. He also had his cars fitted with armor for protection and commissioned the secret construction of elaborate incendiary devices. He had modernized the private airstrip left over from the Second World War when the property had been taken over by the military.

Biz was fascinated to find her intuition about Lord Dawson's character had proved correct. She read that he had studied firearms and dynamite for many years, and had become an expert in their use. As a youth, he learned as much as he could about them and practiced shooting on the family's private range. He even experimented with explosives on the estate when his parents were not around, sending metal flying both up in the air and over land hundreds of feet. They soared over his fields before falling to the earth in great crashes, exploding loudly on impact.

He had led this double life for many years and slept soundly despite having many dreadful secrets. And in a twist that made Biz's stomach churn, evidence was found that Lord Dawson had killed his first wife, Helena, when she uncovered his malicious activities, disapproved of them, and wanted to tell the authorities.

Lord Dawson faced significant legal challenges. Clare left him immediately after his arrest, and wanted to sell her Newland Gallery to Arthur, if he could be persuaded. She expected to divorce her husband and move to America by herself, a move she had been contemplating for a long time.

But the news made Biz nervous. If Arthur took ownership of the gallery, he might stay in London.

It was a mild and sunny day for February. By Valentine's Day, Arthur was staying with Biz in America, and they celebrated her birthday by hiking up the trail in New Jersey she so dearly loved. She was already looking forward to a special dinner they planned to have in New York that night, and was building a fine appetite. A slight breeze blew a tiny wisp of hair across her face, and she pulled it aside as she led him energetically along the sunny path.

Trailing not far behind in his hiking boots, Arthur breathed in fresh air with enthusiasm.

Biz had gradually grown more certain Arthur would be the one for her, and she became cautiously optimistic about her future with him. While a career had a place of importance central in her life, it was not the entire point. She would probably stay with WYN-TV for a few more years but the questions of her career and future didn't hang on her so heavily anymore…Arthur had become a sweet dream to her and she gradually became more content with him and within herself. She had a change of heart, and accepted her life as it was, her achievements and her plans, for the time being.

"Let's stop for a minute. Here's a nice place," he said. They approached a rocky ledge and gazed at the stunning view. "I'm sorry I couldn't be with you in Greece when I had to attend to some family business in London," he said. "You see, years ago, my parents didn't want to have much to do with Westland Castle, or the family business and properties, except to help my grandmother sell the real estate and furnishings. After my grandfather died, they were mostly sold to a developer, fortunately, at the height of real estate prices. One of them in London is now the new location of the Chaucerian Club. Anyway, my grandmother did little with the money from the estate except to invest it conservatively. In a nutshell, the amount she left me after her estate was settled, the taxes paid and properties sold, is far more generous than I expected, as I heard recently in London.

"I would say we deserve each other," he continued. "Though in some ways we're only beginning to learn about each another. I promise you, I'll do my very best for you. We can live wherever we want. A certain white lace dress might be useful…"

She looked at him, confused.

"In other words," he blushed. "Please, will you marry me?"

As he asked, he reached into his pocket and handed her a blue velvet box he had carried to America with a diamond ring inside.

Biz, eager and willing, agreed in a heartbeat. She absolutely would allow him to ride the waves of life with her, and knew she would benefit from it in many ways. She marveled at how the basic emotions of men and women had hardly changed at all through many centuries of human existence.

It was a heady feeling for both of them as they recognized the strength of their mutual feelings for each other. Whatever the obstacle, they would find a solution no matter what. Secure in each other's arms, they gazed serenely at Surprise Lake as they planned their futures together forever.

Acknowledgments

This manuscript would not have been published without the key advice and assistance I have been fortunate to have received from many colleagues, friends and relatives. They gave me encouragement and without them the book would have been very different, and might not have been completed and published. I also have to thank old friends who provided me with inspiration. Writing this story has brought back memories of places in my past that I wanted to remember and revisit. It was a pleasure to create, research, and write.

Jim Lebbad of *Lebbad Design* created the cover and logo, offered encouragement, and referred me to other publishing professionals.

Joy Stocke of *Wild River Consulting and Publishing*, my conceptual editor, expressed her belief in me and my manuscript. Without her, the story would have been very different. I have to thank her for her attention and professional skill and for relentlessly encouraging me to keep going.

Nina Alvarez of *Dream Your Book*, my story coach and line editor, I have to attempt to thank for her constant availability and responsiveness and all she did, always with a positive upbeat attitude to correct my multiple errors. She worked hours upon hours cutting, correcting, and changing pages, and I can't thank her enough. I am very grateful for her attention and impressed at her thoroughness and professional work ethic.

Fay Sciarra at *faysciarra.com*, a gifted artist and former television producer, is to be thanked for informing me about both art and television production.

Kim Nagy of *Wild River Review* generously offered useful information about the publishing industry.

Foremost, I have to give credit to my family: Amy, Emily, and especially Paul, without whom I would not have gained the experience and confidence I needed. I wish for all of their dreams and aspirations to come true.

Amy Seymour has been consistently helpful with substantial editorial and technical support. She solved challenges posed by several story conflicts, and patiently listened to me reflect on the plot.

Emily Seymour was extremely influential in supporting my basic belief in the story's ideas. She jointly created the spine of the story with me and supported the idea that it could be transformed into a book people would read. I would also like to thank her for solving certain story conflicts, and for listening.

Paul Seymour, an experienced mathematical writer, listened to my ideas and supported me with the time, places, and computers to write.

For these, and for many other advisers who listened to me talk about my manuscript and encouraged me, who were not named perhaps because they did not wish me to name them but are not forgotten, please accept my gratitude. To all, I will remain forever grateful. I couldn't have done it without you.

Thanks, finally, I extend to my readers. Without the prospect of readership, this book most likely would not have been published.